THE BILLIONAIRE IN HER BED

THE BILLIONAIRE IN HER BED

REGINA KYLE

Hannah,

Happy reading!

Regina

This book is a work of fiction. Names, characters, places, and incidents are the product of the author's imagination or are used fictitiously. Any resemblance to actual events, locales, or persons, living or dead, is coincidental.

Entangled Publishing, LLC
2614 South Timberline Road
Suite 105, PMB 159
Fort Collins, CO 80525
rights@entangledpublishing.com

Indulgence is an imprint of Entangled Publishing, LLC.

Edited by Candace Havens
Cover design by Liz Pelletier
Cover art from iStock

Manufactured in the United States of America

First Edition September 2017

To the real-life David and Chris. Your real-life love story is better than anything I could ever write. Thanks for setting the bar so high.

Chapter One

A homeless guy taking refuge from the cold at the far end of the bar with a shot of Fireball whiskey, two twenty-somethings who looked like they'd accidentally wandered into a war zone, and Wayne, Flotsam and Jetsam's answer to Norm from *Cheers*.

Yep. Another hopping Tuesday night in Sunset Park West, Brooklyn.

Not.

"That's it for you." Brooke Worthington snatched away Wayne's empty beer bottle before he could ask for another. "Time to go home. Is your wife on the way, or should I get you an Uber?"

"Uber," he croaked, his breath smelling like stale cigarettes and his preferred brand of cheap beer.

Her shift couldn't end soon enough.

She grabbed a towel and a spray bottle of disinfectant from beneath the bar and started to scrub the scarred oak surface. "Go to the bathroom and freshen up. I'll take care of the car."

He let out a loud burp and wiped his mouth on his sleeve. Gross. "Thanks, Brooke. You're too good to me."

"Don't I know it." She waved him away. "Go. Before I change my mind and call your wife."

"You wouldn't." He teetered on his stool, grabbing the bar rail to keep from falling.

She arched a brow at him. "Wouldn't I?"

He eased himself off the stool with all the grace of a spastic walrus and tottered toward the bathroom. Brooke went back to the task at hand, holding her breath against the strong smell of the disinfectant.

Probably a holdover from all the time she'd spent sitting in hospital rooms, waiting for Mallory to finish chemo or radiation. To this day, she associated the smell of ammonia with sickness. Ammonia and anxiety, with a side order of dried blood and unwashed feet, saturating the air like an old sponge. It gave her the willies.

"Excuse me."

A deep, husky voice conjured images of naked bodies, sweaty and entwined, stopping her rag mid-swipe. Had it been so long since she'd had sex that some random guy's Barry White impression was all it took to shift her brain into bad porno mode? She mentally tallied up the days, which quickly multiplied into months. And months. And months.

Yep. It had.

She raised her head, ready to feast her eyes on the holder of the voice that had her girly parts doing the Macarena, and her breath caught in her throat. If she hadn't been holding on to the bar for dear life, she would have crumpled onto the beer-stained floor like Wayne almost taking a header off his barstool, except she would have been more of a puddle of lust than a drunken heap.

Tall. Christ, he was tall. Probably six-one or six-two, and every inch of him long, lean, and lip-smacking. She let her gaze linger on his magnificently manly chest and impossibly broad shoulders before traveling up to his chiseled jaw, dotted with the perfect amount of sexy stubble. Dark hair fell in waves over his brow, and piercing Paul Newman-blue eyes stared out at her from under sinfully long lashes.

Figures. The first guy worth a second, third, and fourth look to walk into Flotsam and Jetsam, and she was up to her elbows in cleaning solution.

"Do you have a phone I could use?" He shoved his hands in the pockets of his cashmere coat, which he wore over a crisp, white button-down shirt that looked right at home with his pleated charcoal dress pants. "I left mine back at the office."

"Uh, sure." Phone. Shit. She'd forgotten Wayne's Uber. She threw the towel in the sink, squirted some hand sanitizer onto her palms, and reached for her cell on the shelf behind the bar. "Just let me take care of something first."

"No problem." Tall, dark, and scruffy sat his oh-so-fine butt onto the stool a few feet down from the one Wayne had vacated. Sexy and smart. Another plus in Mr. Almost Perfect's column. *Almost* because in Brooke's world, no one was the total package. Everyone had warts. Some more than others.

"Can I get you a drink while you wait?" She tapped the Uber app on her phone and entered the required information. Type of vehicle, pickup location, destination—which she unfortunately knew all too well, having requested rides for Wayne more times than she could count. "On the house."

"Are you sure this place can afford to give booze away?" His eyes darted around the virtually empty bar. "Your boss might not approve."

She lifted a shoulder. "What he doesn't know won't hurt him."

"Then I'll take a Macallan. Neat."

"You're kidding, right?" She closed the app and slid her

cell across the bar to him. "I've got Dewar's and Johnnie Walker Black."

"Make it a Johnnie Walker." He ran a hand through his thick, disheveled locks, pushing them off his face for a nanosecond before they flopped back over his forehead. "Is it always this dead in here?"

"On Tuesdays in January, yeah." She snagged a fresh towel, sprayed some disinfectant on it, and gave the bar top another wipe down. "Hopefully business will pick up once the new Fairway opens down the street."

"New Fairway?" He picked up her phone and started to dial. "I didn't know they were setting up shop here."

"They're breaking ground in the spring." She stowed the disinfectant under the bar and wiped her hands on the towel before chucking it into the sink with the first one. "What are you, some sort of supermarket groupie?"

"Not exactly." He frowned at the phone.

"No answer?"

"Straight to voicemail." He slid it back to her. "Better than the alternative, I suppose."

"What's the alternative?" She stuck her phone in her bra.

He grimaced. "You don't want to know."

"I can call you a cab. Or get you an Uber." Like Wayne. Where was he, anyway? His car should be pulling up any minute.

"How about that drink first?" He smiled, showing two rows of blindingly white, perfectly straight teeth that had no doubt made some orthodontist a fortune, and a set of dimples guaranteed to drive women crazy.

"Coming right up." She plunked a rocks glass down on the bar in front of him and took the bottle of Johnnie Walker from the shelf behind her. "You're not from around here, are you?"

The expensive haircut. The crisply pressed pants. The

whole Macallan thing. It all reeked of the island. This guy was a Manhattanite through and through. Besides, if he were from the neighborhood, she'd know. One advantage of tending bar—pretty much everyone over the legal drinking age stopped in at some point or another.

"You could say that." Mr. Manhattan propped his elbows on the bar and leaned in so she could smell his cologne, orange and cedar, with a hint of patchouli.

No doubt. A city boy. Probably worked on Wall Street or at some Park Avenue law firm. Normally, she avoided his type like the Ebola virus. Rich and entitled, like her father. Like every one of the boys in her snobby, suburban high school. That's why she'd escaped to the cultural melting pot that was Sunset Park.

So why did this guy press all her sexual hot buttons? Was she that desperate to end her cold streak? Heck, even her baby sister was breaking out of her safety zone and dating one of the doctors at the clinic where she volunteered. Mommy and Daddy approved, of course. But at least she was getting some action. That was a hell of a lot more than Brooke could say.

She measured two fingers of scotch into his glass. "So, what brings you to Brooklyn?"

"Work." He didn't elaborate, just sipped his scotch. Even that was a turn-on, the way his Adam's apple bobbed in the smooth, strong column of his throat. "What about you? What's a nice girl like you doing in a place like this?"

She bent over and rested her forearms on the bar, bringing her face inches from his. Her pathetic attempt at flirting—not exactly her strong suit—for once seemed to be paying off. Heat crackled between them, and she fought the urge to see if his jaw felt as deliciously rough under her fingertips as she imagined. "Who said I was nice?"

"Hey, Brooke." Leave it to Wayne to pick the most inopportune moment to reappear. A streamer of toilet paper trailed from his shoe. Talk about a mood killer. "My Uber here yet?"

She extracted her phone from between her breasts and swiped the screen. "Looks like he's pulling up now. Silver Toyota Prius."

"Thanks." He took his coat from the back of his barstool and toddled toward the exit. "See you tomorrow, doll."

"Not if I see you first," she quipped to his back as he vanished through the door.

Her mystery man studied her over the top of his glass. "Friend of yours, Brooke?"

Her name rolled off his tongue and over his full, kissable lips like sweet, syrupy music, an aphrodisiac that had her body humming like a tuning fork. "Regular. And thanks to him, you've got an unfair advantage over me."

He tilted his head to one side. "How so?"

She stuck her phone in the back pocket of her suede mini skirt. "You know my name, but I don't know yours."

"Eli." Again, he didn't embellish, and she liked that. Short. Simple. To the point.

"Last call," she announced loudly for the sake of the three lost souls left in the place, not counting her and her new friend Eli.

He tapped the rim of his glass. "Might as well hit me again before you throw me out."

She poured him two more fingers of whiskey, nodding to the twenty-somethings on their way out before turning her attention back to her intended target.

"I could use some company while I clean up. It gets awfully lonely around here after closing time."

Ohmigod. Did she seriously just say that? No one would ever accuse her of being shy, but sexually aggressive wasn't in her wheelhouse. What had come over her? It was like aliens had taken over body. Horny, sex-starved aliens.

Eli jerked his head toward the end of the bar, where the homeless guy was fast asleep with his Fireball. "What about him?"

"There's a shelter a few blocks over. I'll have a cab drop him off." She took a shot glass, filled it with a liberal portion of Jägermeister, and lifted it halfway to her mouth. Nothing like a little liquid courage to unlock her inhibitions. "So, what do you say? Are you in a rush to get home? Or can you help a girl out?"

"Well, when you put it that way…" He clinked his glass with hers. "Far be it from me to abandon a damsel in distress."

• • •

Eli Ward smiled as he sipped his crappy scotch. Poor quality of the booze aside, things were definitely looking up.

Not hard, considering how his day had started.

His morning joe—black with two shots of espresso—all over the front of his gray and white pinstripe Robert Graham dress shirt? Check. His driver out sick and not an empty cab to be found in SoHo during morning rush hour? Check.

And then, the trifecta. The rancid cherry on top of his shit sundae.

They'd lost the East Harlem project, the latest in a series of business disasters for Momentum Development. An old sugar refinery in Dumbo. A former elementary school in Stuyvesant. An abandoned warehouse in Flatbush. All snatched from under him at the eleventh hour by his biggest rival in the New York City real estate game, Noel Dupree.

Somehow, some way, Dupree was getting the best of him. Eli had made an art of flying under the radar with his projects until it was time to go public. And that meant working with only the most circumspect, trustworthy people. His vetting process was extensive. But not for the first time he wondered if Momentum had a mole. It was the only explanation he could think of for Dupree's recent successes.

Which was why he'd played it closer to the vest with the East Harlem project. The only people in on it were Eli and his best friend and business partner, Simon Adler. Eli had even left his totally trustworthy PA Ginny out of the loop to be on the safe side.

And, in all likelihood, that meant only one thing. His best friend and business partner was selling him out. Exactly how and exactly why, Eli didn't know. But he was going to find out.

To do that, he needed some space. Otherwise he ran the risk of either tipping Simon off that he was wise to him or punching his face in.

So, he'd run—told a shocked and confused Ginny to cancel his meetings and hopped on a subway to anywhere, winding up thirty minutes from Manhattan in Sunset Park. Which, according to the charming, attentive, and extremely attractive Brooke, was soon to be the site of a new Fairway. What developers like him referred to as a green shoot, a harbinger of gentrification and increased property values.

He logged that fact in his brain and moved on to more pressing matters. Like the fetching female across the bar.

He sat back and studied her as she moved about the room, wiping down tables, pushing in chairs, sweeping the floor. Not his usual type, for sure. Instead of sharp angles and hard edges, she was soft and warm and inviting, with curvy hips and a J-Lo booty he was dying to get his hands on. Raven hair fell in lush, dark waves to her shoulders, framing a face that housed a sensuous mouth begging to be kissed.

And to top it all off, like a red, ripe cherry perched on the seriously scrumptious ice cream sundae his day had transformed into, she had absolutely no freaking idea who the hell he was. No clue he was a member of the *Forbes* 400. No chance she was after him for his money or his social status.

She was just a woman—a damned attractive woman—who seemed like she wanted him as much as he did her.

She caught him staring and gave a thick, throaty laugh. His dick twitched in his pants. Fuck, she was a walking, talking wet dream.

His for the taking. No strings attached. The perfect end to an imperfect day.

He knocked back the rest of his shitty scotch, thunked the empty glass down on the bar, and slid off his stool. "Need a hand?"

She shook her head, sending her blue-black tresses swaying around her face like a velvety curtain. "I'm almost done. Have to count out the night's receipts—what little there are—and lock them up in the office safe."

She swapped the broom for the cash drawer and motioned for him to follow her down a narrow hallway off the back of the bar. She stopped in front of an old-fashioned wood-paneled door with a frosted glass window, took a ring of keys from the belt loop of her super-short mini skirt, and inserted one into the lock. "Here we are. My home away from home."

She pushed the door open and flicked on a grainy fluorescent light overhead. He trailed in after her. When he could drag his eyes away from the seductive sway of her generous ass in the skintight mini, he saw she wasn't kidding about the home away from home thing. The office was like a combination kitchen, bedroom, and workspace, complete with a microwave, mini-fridge, and futon in addition to the traditional desk, chair, and filing cabinets.

He opted for the futon, taking a seat and crossing an ankle over his knee. "Nice digs."

She sat behind the desk and started sorting the cash from the drawer. "I spend enough time here. Figured I might as well make it comfortable."

"You own this place?"

"Manager. Bartender. Jack of all trades. It pays the bills." She stuck the money in an envelope, sealed it, and scrawled something across the front. When she was done, she crossed to the safe and knelt to dial in the combination. The door swung open, and she shoved the envelope inside. "There. All set."

She slammed the safe shut and stood. "I have a surprise for you."

"Oh?" One corner of his mouth lifted in a half smile.

"Not that kind of surprise." An adorable flush crept across her cheeks and one finger toyed with the shiny silver infinity knot that hung between her breasts. His seductress was nervous. Somehow that only served to make her more appealing.

She crossed back to the desk, opened the bottom drawer, and produced a bottle of dark, amber liquid with an all-too familiar label.

"I thought you said you didn't carry Macallan."

"We don't." Two shot glasses joined the bottle on the desk. "This is my boss's private stash."

"Won't he notice it's been raided?"

"He won't miss a couple of shots." She poured two fingers in each glass then added an extra splash for good measure. "Besides, he owes me. I've covered for him twice this week."

She came around to the front of the desk and handed him a glass. He smelled then sipped the top-shelf whiskey, taking in only enough to cover the surface of his tongue, then swirling it in his mouth before swallowing and sighing contentedly. "Now that's how scotch is supposed to go down. Smooth, no burn."

"You've got expensive taste."

"I know what I like." He repeated his sip, swirl, and swallow ritual.

"Is that so?" She took a healthy gulp of scotch and set her glass down on the desk behind her. "See anything else you like?"

"Maybe." He snagged her hand, pulling her down onto the futon. She landed half in his lap and half on the seat beside him. The half in his lap pressed against his crotch, making his disobedient dick twitch again. He polished off his drink faster than good scotch deserved, ditched his glass, and ran a hand up the smooth, pale skin of her leg, stopping just under the hem of her skirt. "Tell me you want this as much as I do."

"I want this as much as you do," she echoed in a breathy whisper.

His fingers toyed with the lacy edge of her panties. "Last chance to change your mind."

She sucked in a breath. "Thanks, but no thanks. Carry on."

He lowered his face to hers and spoke next to her ear, ruffling the tendrils of hair at the base of her neck. "Good answer."

He kissed the side of her neck where it met her shoulder, sucking her silky-soft skin into his mouth. She tasted of vanilla and honey, like a rich, exotic confection from some upscale bakery. The sweetness lingered on his tongue and made him hungry for more.

Her head fell back, lifting her beautiful breasts, bringing them that much closer to his greedy mouth.

"Really good," she moaned, echoing his sentiment.

His lips found hers in a kiss that was equal parts desperation and desire. He wanted to devour her right there on the narrow futon in her cramped office.

With a frustrated groan, Brooke straddled his lap, placing her hands on the sides of his face. She deepened the kiss, holding his head at the perfect angle for her to ravage him. He let her take control. Hell, he more than let it happen—he loved it. Loved that she was as wild for him as he was for her. Loved the way she ground against him, making him groan and beg her not to stop.

When he couldn't stand it any longer, he flipped her onto her back. "My turn."

Bracing himself on one elbow, he used his free hand to hike her skirt up.

He traced the strip of seafoam green silk and lace of her thong with his index finger to where it disappeared between the two luscious globes of her ass. "Damn."

"What can I say?" She arched into him, thrusting the sweetly curved mounds of her breasts into his chest. Her nipples strained against her shirt and poked at his pecs. "I'm a sucker for naughty lingerie."

So was he, when she was wearing it. Not that she'd be wearing it for long. Christ, she was as wet as he was hard. He sank a finger into her sweet depths to the knuckle, mimicking what he'd soon be doing with his cock.

She moaned and clenched around him. Her eyes fluttered closed and her lips parted on a soft sigh.

"I spoke too soon." He added a second finger and pumped them in and out, spreading her wide. "This isn't good."

She tensed beneath him, and he lowered his mouth to hers, doing his best to kiss her doubts away.

"It's fan-fucking-tastic."

Chapter Two

Who was this guy, and where had he been her whole life?

Current dry spell notwithstanding, Brooke was no stranger to sex.

But her experience hadn't prepared her for this. For Eli staring down at her as if she were a Christmas present and he was trying to decide how to unwrap her, those piercing, almost translucent blue eyes heating her from the inside out. The fingers inside her curved and penetrated deeper, hitting that secret spot that made her cry out with pleasure.

"Like that, do you?" The cocky bastard had the nerve to chuckle.

A smile played around the corners of her lips. Two could play that game.

"Mm-hmm." She snaked a hand around the back of his neck, pulling him down so her tongue could trace the shell of his ear. She worked her way down to the lobe, taking it between her teeth and giving it a not-too-gentle tug. "How about you? Like that?"

He moaned. "Tease."

"I'm the tease?" She ran her hands down his back, pulling his shirt from his waistband and slipping underneath to touch him. He had way too many clothes on. She'd have to do something about that. Soon. "You're the one making me crazy."

His eyes, heavy-lidded and darkened with desire, met hers. "I'm afraid you'll have to wait a bit longer."

"Jerk."

She writhed underneath him, doing her damnedest to force his fingers deeper inside her. He punished her by withdrawing them entirely.

"You'll be singing a different tune before the night is over."

"Promises, promises."

"That's right." He hooked his thumbs under the strings of her thong. "And I intend to keep them."

She didn't need any coaxing to lift her hips, allowing him to drag her panties down her legs with an excruciating slowness.

"At this rate, we'll be here until dawn."

"What's wrong with that?" He pulled her panties over one foot, then the other. "I don't have anywhere better to be. You?"

"No." She dropped one leg to the floor, opening herself to him. "But I'm worried about Miguel."

He froze with his hand in midair, her panties dangling from one finger. "Boyfriend?"

"Barback. He's on mornings this week." She moistened her lips and trailed a fingernail along his bicep. "I'm afraid we might traumatize him if he walks in on us."

He tossed the thong aside and reached for the hem of her skirt. "We'll lock the door."

"He has a key." She closed a fist around his upper arm. Or tried to. Her fingers barely spanned half the circumference of his meaty bicep.

OMFG. Eli might be a Manhattan yuppie, but he clearly found the time to stay in shape, be it at the gym or running in Central Park or some combination of the above. She shut her eyes and pictured him shirtless and sweaty, fresh from a workout and in need of a hot shower and someone to help scrub his back.

The wet brush of his lips on the sensitive skin behind her knee woke her from her daydream. "Then I guess traumatizing Miguel is a chance we'll have to take."

He shoved at her skirt. She cooperated again, raising her ass so he could hike it up to her waist.

"Now you." She twisted her fingers in the soft fabric of his shirt.

"Fair enough." He helped her yank it over his head, apparently in too much of a hurry to unbutton it. She slid her hands across his chiseled pecs and traveled down his eight-pack, only stopping when she reached the button on his waistband.

He shot to his feet, and for a minute, she thought she'd done something wrong. But then he shucked off his pants and boxer briefs, leaving him gloriously naked. He stretched out on the futon beside her, the hard length of his erection pressing against her belly.

"This has to go." He fingered the neckline of her blouse.

She unfastened the buttons one by one and let the shirt fall open, revealing a sheer seafoam-green bra that matched the thong he'd discarded earlier. "Better?"

"Bra, too," he ordered.

"Bossy." Even as she complained, she found herself reaching around her back to undo the hooks. It was like he was some sort of sexual sorcerer, manipulating her mind and rendering her incapable of disobeying his gruff demand.

He grinned. "You have no idea."

She let the straps drift down her arms, keeping the cups in place with her palms.

"Are you going to stay like that all night?" he asked, running his knuckles over the lacy edge of one cup.

She lowered her hands, letting her bra drop slowly. Without taking his eyes off hers, he picked it up and flung it over his shoulder.

"What did you do that for?"

"I don't want anything between us."

"Oh." Something inside her melted, and she wondered again where this model of manhood had come from and what she'd done to deserve him. He touched her like she was a hothouse flower, fragile and precious.

Reaching down, she encircled him with her fingers. He was hot and hard. His free hand covered hers, moving her palm over the head then down the shaft again. She wrapped one leg over his hips, bringing him closer to her warm, wet, and equally ready center.

"Condom," he growled, rolling away from her to pluck his pants off the floor.

Shit. She was so far gone the thought of protection hadn't entered her lust-clouded mind. Thank God he'd been aware enough to remember. Not that it said much for her powers of seduction.

He pulled his wallet from the back pocket of his pants and fished out a foil packet, holding it up.

Brooke raised herself up on one elbow and let her eyes wander over his body. "Are you going to stand there all day posing, or are you going to get over here?"

"Door number two." He suited up and rejoined her on the futon, pulling her on top of him. "Ride me."

She reached down between them and guided him to her entrance.

"Christ." He ground out the word from the back of his

throat. "You feel so fucking good."

"You, too."

She would have said more, but he took hold of her hips and started moving inside her, at first slowly, then faster, robbing her of coherent thought. With each thrust, she released a small, needy moan. Her head fell back, and her eyes closed as she climbed higher and higher, closer to the edge and her ultimate release.

"I'm…"

"Yes."

"Eli."

"Now."

Every cell in her body vibrated with energy, like she was racing a hundred miles an hour, on fire, toward climax. She arched her back and curled her toes, riding the tsunami.

"Holy hell." Eli's grip on her hips tightened and with a low, guttural groan he thrust into her one last time.

She collapsed on top of him, burying her face against his neck as her chest rose and fell with her deep breaths. They lay like that for a minute, her sweat-drenched body sticking to his. Silent. Awkward. Unsure.

He was the first to stir, rolling them to one side.

"Holy hell," he repeated, scrubbing a hand across his stubbled jaw.

"That bad?" She winced at her lame attempt at a joke.

"You know damn well it wasn't. Fuck, if I had another condom, I'd say let's do it again." He glanced down at his semi-hard cock. "In a few minutes, when I've had time to recover."

"If that's the only thing holding you back, I've got good news for you."

"There's a box of Trojans in the desk drawer?" he asked hopefully.

"No." She gave him what she hoped was a saucy smile, filled both hands with his tight butt, and squeezed. "But there's a condom dispenser in the men's room."

• • •

"You look like crap." Ginny glanced around the hole-in-the-wall diner, taking in the grease-stained walls and ripped pleather seats. "And why did you want to meet me way out here? What's wrong with Dean & Deluca? Or the Starbucks on Eighth and 48th?"

Too close to the office, that's what was wrong. He'd explain as soon as he flagged down a waitress and got what, from the look of the place, was sure to be a crappy cup of coffee.

"Nice to see you, too," Eli quipped, flapping his arms like a madman and finally getting the attention of one of the servers, a frazzled-looking woman in a pale-pink polyester uniform, who looked like she'd stepped right out of central casting for the role of overworked, underpaid food service employee. He ordered two coffees and took the risk of asking for a couple of menus.

"Here." Ginny slid his phone across the table to him.

"Thanks." He slipped it into his pocket. "You're a lifesaver."

"I hope the reason for this little excursion is so you can tell me what's going on." Frown lines creased her forehead. "You've been missing in action for almost two days. I was worried sick."

Guilt clawed at his gut. What an utter shit he'd been, thinking only of himself. While he was off sucking down scotch and screwing bartenders in Sunset Park, Ginny, the only person he could trust, was tearing her thin hair out and losing sleep over him.

He dropped his chin to his chest. "I'm sorry. Really. I didn't mean to freak you out."

"I'm glad you're all right." She leaned over the table

to study him, her bloodshot eyes narrowed. Had she been crying? Because of him? The guilt tightened its grip on his midsection. "You are all right, aren't you?"

"In a manner of speaking."

The waitress chose that moment to show up with their coffees and menus. He waited for her to set them down then went on.

"Can I trust you?" After everything he'd been through the last forty-eight hours he had to ask. For his sanity.

"Of course." She sat back and crossed her legs, emptying a creamer and a packet of sugar into her coffee. "What do you need?"

"I need to lay low for a while," he said, dropping his voice for some unknown reason. It wasn't as if he was likely to run into Simon—or anyone else he knew, for that matter—in Brooklyn at eight a.m. on a Thursday. Or any day. He'd had a hard enough time convincing the usually unquestioning Ginny to make the trek across the East River. "And I want to do it here."

She waved a hand around the restaurant. "In a run-down diner?"

"No." He sipped his coffee. Just as he'd suspected. Crap. But bad coffee was better than no coffee. He took another sip and grimaced. So much for that theory. "In Sunset Park."

Her frown lines deepened. "Why Sunset Park?"

He pushed away his cup and explained the plan that formed the minute a certain sexy barkeep made an offhand comment about the Fairway. It had taken a temporary backseat to getting in her pants—well, skirt, technically—but the next morning, once she'd hustled him out the door before Miguel showed up, it started percolating again as he roamed the streets of the Brooklyn neighborhood.

The supermarket wasn't the only new development popping up. He'd walked past a frozen yogurt shop, a farmto-table restaurant, and an upscale coffeehouse. That added up to one thing in Eli's business brain—dollar signs, provided he could get in on the ground floor before property values went through the roof. He'd even found the perfect project on his sojourn—a former factory someone had chopped up into a handful of loft apartments before going belly up and abandoning the job.

"So, let me get this straight," Ginny said when he was done. "You want to buy an old candy factory in Sunset Park and turn it into luxury condos."

"Right."

"And you want me to help you."

"Right."

"Without letting Simon know what you're doing."

"Right."

"And the reason for all this secrecy is..." She let the sentence hang in the air between them, waiting for him to fill the void.

Eli hesitated, torn. He shared pretty much everything with his administrative assistant. In the eight years she'd worked for him, the matronly woman had become more than his PA. She was the mother he'd never really had, one who made sure he ate three squares a day and brushed his teeth after every meal and got at least eight hours of sleep. Or tried to.

But admitting he'd been stabbed in the back by his best friend? That wasn't something he ready to discuss, even with Ginny. The wounds were still too raw.

"Business?" she prompted when he didn't answer. "Personal?"

"Both," he admitted. "I think Momentum has a mole."

Ginny choked on her coffee. "Are you serious?"

"As an eviction notice." He handed her a napkin. "It's the only way Dupree could have known about Dumbo. And Stuyvesant. And Flatbush."

"Who?" She dabbed her mouth and balled up the napkin in her fist. "Simon? "

"I don't know." The list of suspects was short, but he wasn't ready to call it. Not out loud, not until he had proof. Which was why he'd dragged Ginny out to the boroughs. "But I'm going to find out."

"How are you going to do that if you're playing recluse in Brooklyn?"

"That's where you come in." He paused for the waitress, who was hovering over him with her pad and pen at the ready for their orders. Ginny got oatmeal with raisins and he settled on scrambled eggs and bacon, which he figured even the worst short-order cook couldn't screw up. When the waitress snapped her pad closed and turned on the heel of her non-slip shoes, he continued. "I need you to be my eyes and ears at the office while I'm quietly working this Sunset Park deal. Keep me in the loop. Keep things running smoothly."

"Done," Ginny said without taking even a beat to consider her answer.

"And you'll have to watch my penthouse. Water my plants. Forward my mail."

"Where to?"

He pushed a piece of paper with an address scrawled on it across the table. "I've got a month-to-month lease for an apartment at Candy Court."

It hadn't been easy tracking down the listing agent, getting a hold of the owner, and negotiating a lease in less than two days. But Eli was determined. And when he was determined, shit got done.

"Candy Court?" Ginny unfolded the paper and studied it.

"The building I'm going to buy. And trust me, the name will be the first thing to go. Figured I could kill two birds with one stone. Hide out and do some recon."

"What am I supposed to tell Simon when he asks for

you?" She refolded the paper and tucked it safely into the purse at her feet. "And your sister?"

Shit. His sister. How could he have forgotten her? Paige might be buried in work as a postdoc research fellow at Columbia, but that didn't mean he could go AWOL without her noticing. She had an annoying habit of dropping by his place unannounced, usually to raid the fridge or do a few loads of laundry.

"I'll deal with Paige. And I couldn't care less what you tell Simon. Tell him I'm at a monastery in Tibet. On a sailboat in the Caribbean. Hiking the Appalachian Trail."

"Fine," Ginny huffed. "I'll come up with a suitable cover story on my own. How long will you be in hiding?"

He shrugged. "A few weeks. A few months. However long it takes to figure out who's doing this."

Someone—most likely Simon, unless his partner had shot off his mouth and told someone else about the East Harlem project—was fucking with his livelihood. With the business he'd built with his blood, sweat, and tears. And once he smoked them out, they were going down.

Hard.

Chapter Three

"All right, everyone. Take a seat." Brooke raised her voice a notch so Mr. Feingold, who was notorious for forgetting to wear his hearing aids, could hear her at the back of the room. "I call this meeting of the Candy Court Tenants' Association to order."

"I don't understand why we're still meeting if we're not going to be living here much longer," protested Charise, the hairdresser who lived across the hall with her infant son. Little Jaden must be with his grandmother, since he wasn't where he usually was during their meetings—strapped to his mother's chest.

"We don't know how long it will take the building to sell," Brooke explained. "Or what the new owner will do. Until then, it's business as usual."

"What's going to happen to our community garden?" asked David. The concert pianist lived downstairs from Brooke with his partner, Chris, a professional ballet dancer—the two hottest guys in a ten-mile radius, with the exception of a certain sexy, scotch-drinking stranger.

Her encounter, for lack of a better word, with Eli had been a blip on the radar screen of her sex life. A hell of a pleasurable blip. She'd lived in a sort of sensual stupor for days afterward. Now it was back to normal. Which for her meant work, work, more work, and wrangling the Candy Court residents for their monthly meeting.

"We'll get to the garden." She held up a sheet of paper. "It's number two on the agenda. First, I'd like to hear about any maintenance issues you're having."

"Looks like chicken scratch to me," Mr. Feingold grumbled, causing his wife, sitting next to him on the repurposed sofa Brooke had rescued from the curb and restored, to jab him in the ribs. He glared at her and rubbed his side. "Ouch."

Brooke flipped the paper over so she could read it. Not chicken scratch, thank you very much. Her most recent artwork for the graphic novel she'd been perfecting for the better part of the last six months. With any luck, her agent would give this latest round of edits a thumbs-up and start sending it out to publishers. Brooke exchanged it for the computer-generated agenda on her drafting table. "Sorry. Wrong one."

"What's the point of listing our grievances?" Chris set a plate of spring rolls on the counter that separated the kitchen and dining area from the living area, next to the chips, dip, and salsa from the other tenants. He and David always brought the best food. And booze, she thought as David added a growler of craft beer from the brewery around the corner. "Who's going to fix anything? We've got no super."

True. Floyd had been lucky enough to find a new gig and new housing within weeks of the FOR SALE sign going up in front of Candy Court, moving on along with a bunch of the other tenants. That left only four apartments occupied—her and Charise on the third floor, Chris and David and the Feingolds on the second. Even the retail space on the first floor was vacant.

Brooke's stomach growled, a casualty of not eating since the half a cinnamon raisin bagel she'd had for breakfast at six. David plucked a spring roll from the plate his partner had set down, placed it on a cocktail napkin, and handed it to her. She nodded her thanks. "It couldn't hurt to present a list of demands to the landlord."

"Couldn't help much, either," Mr. Feingold grumbled again, earning him another elbow jab.

"Our kitchen sink is leaking," his wife offered. "And there's a loose tile in the shower."

"My washing machine is acting up again," Charise added, snagging one of the spring rolls.

"The pilot light on our gas stove keeps going out," Chris called from the counter, where he was pouring himself a beer.

"Slow down, slow down." Brooke put the agenda aside and grabbed a clipboard and pen. "Kitchen sink, shower tile, washing machine, pilot light. And the screen in my bedroom window is torn. Anything else?"

Her question was met with silence.

"Good," David said after a few beats. "Now can we talk about the garden?"

"Okay." Brooke tapped the clipboard with her pen. "Moving on to agenda item number two. Before the first frost, we managed to get all our planter boxes set up on the roof. Special thanks to the Feingolds for getting the lumber donated."

"Happy to do it," said Mrs. Feingold.

"Do what?" her husband asked, his already wrinkled brow wrinkling further. "What did you do now?"

"Not me, us," his wife corrected. "Let this be a lesson. Maybe next time you'll remember your hearing aids so you'll know what people are saying about you."

Mr. Feingold muttered something about not wanting

to hear ninety percent of what people had to say, anyway. Brooke swallowed a laugh and pressed on. "Our next order of business is to decide what we're going to grow and how much."

"Again, I don't understand why we're bothering to talk about this," Charise mumbled through a mouthful of spring roll. "Odds are whoever buys this place is going to tear it down. And even if by some miracle he doesn't, the garden's a goner for sure. Then all our hard work will be for nothing."

"It's not nothing," Brooke insisted, relieved to see the others nodding in agreement. "Until someone tells us otherwise, this is still our home. We can't stop living because the building is on the market. Life is filled with uncertainty. We can't let it control us."

"Hear, hear." Chris raised his glass in a silent toast then drank.

"Well said," David agreed, scooping guacamole onto a paper plate with a tortilla chip.

"What did she sa—ouch." Mr. Feingold narrowed his eyes at his wife, who had apparently jabbed him again. "I'm warning you, woman. One more jab, and I'll..."

"So," Brooke interrupted, her forced cheer making her sound like Carol Brady on helium. "Now that we've decided to move forward, what are we going to plant?"

She held a hand up to the older man, who had opened his mouth to speak. "And before you suggest it, Mr. Feingold, we are not growing medical marijuana, no matter how much it helps your glaucoma."

"Cucumbers. I love cucumbers."

"Bibb lettuce. And zucchini."

"Cucumbers and zucchini take up too much room. We should start with something small, like carrots. Or bell peppers."

"Peppers give me gas."

"I think we should grow something pretty, like nasturtiums."

"How about an herb garden?"

The suggestions came fast and furious. Brooke ignored the intermittent squabbling and colorful asides—TMI on the gas, Mr. Feingold—and scribbled each one down.

"I'm partial to peas myself," a new but oddly familiar voice added to the list. The rough, sexy growl that had haunted her every waking moment—and most of her unconscious ones, too—sent pinpricks of awareness flickering down her spine. "Or hibiscus, if you'd rather go the floral route."

Brooke's pen slowed, and she lifted her head. Eli stood in the open door, as scrumptious as she remembered him, his chestnut hair dusted with snow that the forecasters had been predicting all week and his face as unreadable as the sphinx.

"So." His lips curled into a half-smile, and he ruffled his hair, sending flurries fluttering to the floor. "We meet again."

• • •

Fate was a fickle bitch.

Why else would the woman who'd spent the last few days running naked through Eli's mind be standing in front of him fully clothed now, presiding over a tenants' meeting in the very building he planned to grab up and gut?

Said woman lowered her clipboard and pen. Her emerald eyes spat darts of green fire at him. "How did you get in here? And what do you want?"

"Door was open." He held up a canary yellow flyer. "I found this by the mailboxes. Something about an association meeting."

"I made that." An older woman piped up from the sofa. "On the computer. My son-in-law taught me how to use Photostop."

"I think you mean Photoshop." A well-dressed man holding a plate of cheese and crackers corrected her.

"Read it again." Brooke ignored them both, her eyes, still full of flames, never leaving Eli. "It says tenants' association. As in people who live here."

"Meet the new resident of 3-C." He jingled a ring of keys. "Howdy, neighbor."

"You know this place is for sale, right?" a stunning young African-American woman asked. "We could get booted out of here with barely any notice."

Eli flashed what he hoped was a charm-their-pants-off smile. Brooke was clearly none too happy to see him. He couldn't afford to have the rest of the tenants ganging up on him before he had a chance to get the lay of the land. "I like to live dangerously."

And he couldn't think of anything more dangerous than sharing a residence with the star of all his new favorite fantasies.

"What's the matter?" Brooke set her clipboard and pen on an antique wooden drafting table. Was she an architect as well as a bartender? Or maybe an artist? With her boho chic vibe he could totally picture her standing before an easel, deep in concentration, a brush in her mouth and streaks of paint in her hair and on her cheeks. He imagined coming up behind her and turning her in his arms, removing the paintbrush from her between her ripe, rosy lips so he could…

"Things not dangerous enough for you in Manhattan?" she asked, jolting him out of his erotic daydream.

"Manhattan?"

His stomach lurched, and he tightened his grip on the strap of the duffel bag slung over his shoulder. Did she know who he was? Or why he was there? Was that why she was less than thrilled to see him? "What makes you think I'm a city boy?"

She rolled her eyes at him. "Have you looked in the mirror lately? You're like a walking advertisement for Fifth Avenue."

Shit. He did a mental tally of the contents of his duffel. Designer shirts. Custom-tailored pants. Cashmere sweaters. Hell, even his underwear had a designer label. He'd have to send Ginny on a shopping spree if he didn't want to blow his cover. Where did regular guys buy clothes, anyway? Target? Wal-Mart? Paige and her postdoc pals swore by Goodwill. Not that his sister wanted for money. He made sure of that, had ever since their parents were killed in a car accident when he was finishing up at Wharton and she was still in high school. She said it was all about the thrill of the hunt, finding an elusive diamond among the cubic zirconia.

Struck by sudden inspiration, he flashed his charming smile again, this time directing its full wattage at Brooke. "You'd be surprised what you can find at Goodwill if you're persistent enough."

She studied him for a few seconds, then shrugged and popped a piece of cheese into her mouth. Eli relaxed his white-knuckle grip on the bag, and the knot in his stomach loosened, too. He'd dodged a bullet and managed to throw her off the track for the time being. But he'd have to be a damn sight more careful in the future if he wanted to stay on the down low. He made a mental note to text Ginny.

"I take it you two know each other, but the rest of us haven't had the pleasure." Cheese and crackers guy held out his free hand. Eli could have kissed him for changing the topic, if he didn't think it would send the wrong message. "I'm Chris. Welcome to the neighborhood."

"And I'm David." A slightly shorter but equally good-looking man came up beside Chris, slipping an arm around his waist. "Chris's partner. We're in 2-A."

Eli nodded to David and shook Chris's hand. "Eli Ward."

At least he could use his name without setting off any alarm bells. Real estate developers weren't exactly rock stars.

"I'm Charise. 3-D. Here." She handed him a red Solo cup. "Have a beer."

"Thanks." He took it and drank, more for the sake of being polite than being thirsty. Cheap beer, like cheap scotch, wasn't exactly his drink of choice. But instead of being assaulted by stale, cardboard crap, his taste buds were awash with flavors. He took another sip, savoring this time instead of slugging. Smooth and heavy-bodied, with great coffee notes throughout and a hint of something else on the back end he couldn't quite identify. "Not bad."

"Vanilla coffee stout." Vanilla. That was the mystery ingredient. David lifted his own cup. "From the brewery around the corner."

A brewery. Eli added that nugget to his mental checklist of reasons to invest in Sunset Park.

Brooke cleared her throat for attention. "Okay, people. As exciting as our new addition is, we're still in the middle of a meeting here."

"We can deal with the garden later. I want to hear more about Eli." An older woman eyed him appraisingly from the sofa. The gray-haired man next to her blew a loud raspberry, but she continued, undeterred. "I don't see a ring on your finger. Tell me, young man, do you have a girlfriend?"

"Or a boyfriend?" asked David, the arm around Chris tightening.

"I'm straight," Eli assured him, then directed his gaze at Brooke. "And single."

She ignored him and started in on the bean dip.

"Oh, what a pity." The older woman *tsked* her disapproval. "A handsome young man like you should have someone to come home to."

"Get a dog," the man next to her suggested. "Less

expensive than a woman, and they never talk back."

"Or cook dinner," said the woman next to him, who Eli had figured out must be his wife. "Or do your laundry. Or..."

"See what I mean about talking back?" Her husband pushed his wire-rimmed glasses up the bridge of his nose. "Dog's definitely the way to go."

"About the garden..." Brooke tried again.

"Is it true, what Chris said?" Charise piped up. "Do you and Eli really know each other?"

"Were you two an item?" David asked, jumping on the way-too-personal bandwagon.

"Despite what you all seem to think, this is not Melrose Place." Brooke adopted a Wonder Woman power pose, hands balled into fists on her hips and feet planted firmly apart. "And I am not sharing the details of my private life at a tenants' meeting."

"How about you, Eli?" Chris needled. "Care to enlighten us?"

Not in a trillion years. A gentleman didn't kiss and tell. Or fuck and tell, as the case may be. He looked to Brooke, his eyes pleading for assistance.

With an exasperated sigh, she took a piece of paper from the drafting table, crumpled it up and tossed it over her shoulder. "Since no one seems interested in discussing anything on the agenda, I declare this meeting adjourned."

Chapter Four

What part of one-night stand did this guy not get?

Brooke's steps slowed as she approached her apartment door. Eli lounged against the frame, balancing two paper cups that bore the logo of the coffee shop on the next block.

She'd successfully avoided running into him for two full days since he crashed the tenants' meeting. No small feat considering he lived down the hall, his door only a few feet from hers.

It helped that she hadn't had to go to work at the bar. She'd asked for some time off and spent it chained to her drafting table, trying to meet a self-imposed deadline. Maybe this would be the year she finally sold her novel. The year her father finally saw her as more than a flighty dreamer who spent her days doodling and her nights doling out alcohol.

Eli held one of the cups out to her, looking hotter than any man had a right to in tight jeans and a Metallica T-shirt. More casual than his usual GQ style, but it totally worked on him. Of course, he'd probably look as mouth-watering in a burlap sack. He was the kind of guy who could wear pretty much anything well. "We need to talk."

"About what?" she asked, feigning ignorance. She took the cup from his outstretched hand and sipped. Hot, strong, and dark, just the way she liked it. Apparently mind reading was one of Eli's many skills, along with charming his way into month-to-month leases and giving world-class orgasms.

"You sure you want to get into it out here?" He glanced at Charise's door.

Damn. He had a point. As much as she didn't trust herself to be alone with him in the close quarters of her studio apartment without jumping his bones, she didn't want all of Candy Court knowing the intimate details of her until recently nonexistent sex life.

"Fine." She juggled the coffee cup in one hand and dug her keys out of her purse with the other. "You can come in. But only for a few minutes. I've got work to do."

She opened the door, and he followed her in. "Charise says you're some sort of cartoonist."

"Graphic novelist," Brooke corrected, tossing her pocketbook onto an overstuffed chair and stripping off her coat. "And Charise has a big mouth."

"Graphic novels, eh? You mean like comic books?"

Eli made himself right at home, lowering himself onto the couch with an easy grace befitting a man of leisure or a member of the British royal family. She wondered, not for the first time, exactly who this guy was and what he did for a living, then she smacked down the flicker of curiosity. It didn't matter who he was or how the hell he made ends meet, because she was not—repeat, *not*—getting involved with him. Relationships were for other people, ones who wanted stuff like marriage. Kids. A brick colonial with a picket fence and two rowdy Labs with a special fondness for the mailman. Things that weren't even glimmers on her horizon.

She had a five-year plan—get an agent and a multibook contract so she could quit tending bar to write and draw full-time. She'd accomplished the first, signing with her agent shortly before Christmas, but she was still working on numbers two and three. And she wasn't going to let any man, no matter how panty-meltingly gorgeous he was, steer her off track. No way, no how. She'd learned from her mother's mistakes.

"No, I don't mean like comic books." Brooke slammed her cup down on the counter with more force than necessary, sloshing coffee on the red-brown granite. "Graphic novels are a lot longer, with more complex plots."

Eli held his palms out in surrender. "I didn't mean to offend."

"Apology accepted." She grabbed a sponge from the sink and mopped up her mess, more to cover how guilty she felt for snapping at him than from any burning desire to clean. She had a hard time remembering that not every question about her career was a dig, and not every man her judgmental father. "But I'm guessing you didn't come here to talk about my work, did you?"

"You guess right." He patted the cushion next to him. "Come sit down."

She shook her head. "No, thanks.

He folded his arms. "I'm not talking to you from across the room."

She lobbed the sponge into the sink and leaned back against the counter. "Then I guess you're not talking."

"If Mohammad won't come to the mountain…" He stood and took a step toward her.

She raised a hand. "Stop right there."

"I don't think so." Step.

"I mean it." She stuck her hand out farther.

"So do I." Step.

"Not an inch more."

Step. "Too late."

He held her gaze as he put a hand on her outstretched arm, slowly lowering it.

"What do you want?" The words came out on a puff of air, like he was stealing her breath with his nearness.

"I told you." He braced a palm against the granite on one side of her, bringing his hard, hot body so close she could see the tiny steel-gray flecks in his blue eyes and the hint of razor burn under his chin. "To talk."

"This doesn't feel like talking."

His low, husky laugh reverberated through her. "What does it feel like?"

Heaven.

"One night." She stared at a spot over his shoulder, desperate for something to distract her from the overwhelming scent of him, soap and sandalwood and sweat. No dice. "It was supposed to be one night."

"Do you believe in fate?" His warm breath danced across her cheek and tickled her ear. "Because it seems to be telling us otherwise."

No, she didn't. She believed in hard work and perseverance. Why else would she still be banging her head against the wall trying to get a top-drawer publisher interested in her novel?

She went for sarcastic, hoping it would scare him off. "Maybe it's telling me you're a stalker."

"Who doesn't know your last name yet somehow found out where you live and rented an apartment in your building?"

She gave a half-hearted shrug. "Could happen."

"Or it could be when I met you that night at Flotsam and Jetsam I was apartment hunting, and I was as surprised to see you at the tenants' meeting as you were to see me. Call it a happy coincidence."

"I don't believe in coincidence, either."

"What do you believe in?" His baby blues, mysterious

and mesmerizing, bored into hers. "Luck?"

She broke free from his spellbinding gaze, dragging her eyes down to his awe-inspiring chest and focusing on the fire-engine red "ALL" in the center of his Metallica T-shirt. "Luck is when preparation meets opportunity."

"Then it looks like this is my lucky day."

"Why is that?"

"Because this is my opportunity to convince you the universe wants us to spend some time together." He slid a finger under her chin and lifted her face to his. "And I'm prepared to stay right here until you agree."

• • •

He was walking a tightrope across the Grand Canyon without a net.

When Brooke found out who he was and why he was there, she'd have his balls in a vice grip. Big time. Which was reason enough for him to back the fuck off.

So why couldn't he?

It wasn't a sexual thing, although it would be futile to deny that he wanted her. But he wasn't some teenager, unable to control his primal urges. He'd resisted plenty of beautiful women in his day.

No, it wasn't Brooke's obvious physical assets that made her irresistible. It was the fact that, no matter how much the lady did protest, her body language shouted loud and clear that she was attracted to him. Eli Ward, regular Joe. Not Eli Ward, billionaire developer. That was a heady prospect, one he hadn't experienced since hitting it big.

Add to that everything he'd learned about her from the other residents in the two short days he'd been at Candy Court. Unlike Brooke, they'd welcomed him with open arms and hadn't hesitated to tell him all about their favorite neighbor.

How she was the driving force behind the community garden and had been the one to sit with Mrs. Feingold at the hospital when her husband fell and broke his hip. How she'd helped Charise out in a pinch by babysitting her little boy after pulling an eight-hour shift at the bar.

Bottom line: this woman was someone he wanted—no, needed—to get to know better. And if that meant engaging in a slight deception for a short time, until he was on surer footing with her, then that was what he had to do. He only hoped the end would justify the means.

"So." He tilted his head to study her, looking for some sign she was on the verge of giving in to him. "What will it take for you to give me a second chance?"

Brooke opened her mouth to answer, but her response was swallowed up by a chirpy, assertive voice from the door.

"Brooke, dear. I forgot my key, and Morty locked me out again when he went to his tai chi class at the Y."

Eli stepped aside to let Brooke push past him. Their elderly neighbor stood in the doorway with a sly smile and a twinkle in her watchful eyes.

"I'm sorry," the older woman said, not looking the least bit apologetic. "I didn't realize you were…occupied. I'll come back later."

"It's okay, Mrs. Feingold." Brooke rounded the counter into the kitchen area. "I've got your spare right here."

"At least someone around here locks their door," Eli muttered.

Brooke opened a drawer and rummaged around until she held up a shiny silver key on an Angry Birds keychain. "Found it."

"Thank you, dear. I don't know what I'd do without you." Mrs. Feingold crossed to Brooke and took the proffered key. "Now, I'll get out of your way and let you two get back to… whatever it was you were doing."

One look at Brooke's stony face told Eli that wasn't going to happen.

"I was just leaving." He offered his arm to Mrs. Feingold. "I'll walk you out."

She placed her hand in the crook of his elbow and beamed up at him. At least he was capable of making one woman happy, even if she was old enough to be his grandmother.

"Aren't you a gentleman?" she cooed.

Brooke choked back a cough.

"Come on, Mrs. F. You can finish telling me about your grandson's bar mitzvah."

Brooke quirked a brow at him. "Mrs. F.?"

The older woman blushed. "It's his nickname for me. Isn't it adorable?"

"Adorable," Brooke grumbled in grudging agreement. "If not terribly original."

He ignored the dig. "Have any of that rugelach left, Mrs. F.?"

"You bet I do," she gushed. "And I can make us some egg creams, too."

"Sounds delicious."

He got perverse satisfaction from the shocked look on Brooke's face as he escorted Mrs. Feingold out the door. What kind of neighbor did she think he was, anyway?

Only the kind of neighbor that plots to throw his fellow tenants out on the street.

He pushed the thought to the back of his brain. Okay, so none of the current residents of Candy Court were going to be able to afford to stay once he converted the apartments over to luxury condos. But what was he supposed to do? The building was falling apart, despite the tenants' best efforts to keep up with the growing list of repairs. If he didn't step in and take control, someone else would. Someone like Noel Dupree, who didn't give a shit about anything except his bottom line—which meant using substandard materials and shoddy labor to rehab properties that just as often depressed the neighborhoods they were supposed to rejuvenate. Eli wasn't about to let that happen.

Besides, he wasn't a total asshat. He'd make sure everyone landed safely somewhere. One apartment was as good as another, right? Home was more than four walls; it was where the heart was. He'd learned that lesson the hard way after his parents died and left him and Paige with a mountain of debt, forcing them to sell the house they'd grown up in.

And if the Candy Court crew wanted to stay together, he'd figure out a way for that to happen, too. Maybe in another building in Sunset Park. He'd done his homework and checked out the competition. There were several more affordable options in the neighborhood with multiple vacancies. He could work with the tenants, maybe get them a package deal. That way they'd not only stay together, they'd the reap benefits of the revitalization his new development was bound to spur.

His guilty conscience temporarily assuaged, he turned his attention to Mrs. Feingold, nodding and smiling at all the appropriate times as she regaled him with every detail of her grandson's big day. When her story was done and he'd eaten his fill of rugelach and egg cream, he offered to take the spare key back to Brooke. He breathed a silent sigh of relief when Mrs. Feingold declined, insisting that her husband would return it later, probably along with a tin of pastries and maybe an egg cream.

Not that he was afraid to face the feisty bartender-slash-cartoonist—correction, graphic artist. Eli Ward didn't do scared. If it were up to him, he'd barge right back in there and pick up where he left off.

But it wasn't. He could sense that Brooke wasn't ready to continue their little dance. Not yet.

He turned the key in his door. The shitshow that greeted him reminded him how much he had left to do to make the one-room studio habitable. The only thing he'd managed to get set up so far was the double bed in the corner he'd designated as his bedroom. A desk sat half assembled beside it. The rest of the furniture he'd ordered with Ginny's help from Ikea was still piled in boxes in the center of the room—a love seat, a bookshelf, a storage bench that would double as a coffee table, and a set of stacking stools he could use as side tables or extra seating.

Originally, he'd intended to have movers bring some of his stuff over from his Manhattan penthouse. He'd scrapped that not-so-brilliant plan when Brooke called him out on his expensive wardrobe. But even a big boy had to have his toys. Which was why his flat-screen TV and state-of-the-art sound system should be arriving in about—he checked his faux Rolex Submariner, another concession to Brooke's keen eye—half an hour.

He dragged his toolbox out from under the bed and unfolded the instructions for assembling the desk, determined to have at least one more piece of furniture put together before the movers arrived. He'd done his fair share of manual labor flipping houses before Momentum had taken off and he'd moved into the executive suite. How hard could one simple little desk be?

Pretty fucking hard, it turned out. Whoever wrote the damn directions must be a sadistic son of a bitch.

Eli was about to crumple the whole indecipherable thing into a ball and go rogue when his cell rang. He swiped the screen to answer without bothering to check who was calling. No need for that now that he'd blocked his former best friend. Until he'd pinned down the identity of Momentum's mole, there was nothing Simon could say that Eli wanted to hear.

"Ward," he barked, his frustration with the desk bleeding

into his tone.

"What kind of way is that to talk to your baby sister?"

His mood immediately softened, and he sat back on his haunches, letting the useless instruction sheet flutter from his fingers to the floor. "Sorry, Paigey. I thought you were the movers."

"Movers?" He could hear her confusion and concern. "What's going on? Your message on my voicemail was totally incomprehensible."

He gave her the condensed version, skipping the whole Brooke situation and focusing on his suspicions about a mole at Momentum and his plans for Candy Court.

"So, let me get this straight," Paige said when he was done. "Someone may or may not be sabotaging Momentum."

"Right."

"And you think that someone is your business partner."

"Right."

"So, you've gone underground in Brooklyn at a former candy factory that you want to renovate, and you're holed up there until you figure out who's out to get you."

"Not renovate, convert," he clarified. "Into luxury apartments."

"Whatever." He could almost see his sister's eyes rolling. "You don't understand organic chemistry. I don't understand real estate development. That's how our relationship works."

He lowered himself the rest of the way to the floor, pushing aside a plastic bag with nuts and bolts so he could sit. "Point taken."

There was silence on the line for a few seconds then Paige asked, "Can I still do my laundry at your place?"

"You have a key. It's not like I could stop you."

"Thanks." Something rustled over the line, like she was shuffling papers. Was she at the lab? On a Saturday? "I don't have to water your plants, do I? You know I suck at keeping things alive."

"Says the organic chemist."

"So, you do understand organic chemistry."

"Maybe a little," he conceded. Enough to know she'd never lack for work, with her summa cum laude Ivy League degrees. Which was what he wanted for her. Safety. Security. Happiness. The things he'd tried so hard to provide since their parents' deaths.

"You never answered my question."

"No, Paige." Eli rested his head against the wall and closed his eyes. "You don't have to water my plants. That's what I have Ginny for."

"She's your administrative assistant, not your housekeeper."

"She's whatever I need her to be. And right now, that's my everything until I've got this mess at the office sorted out."

"Sometimes you are such an arrogant jerk."

He smiled, eyes still closed. "Part of my charm."

"You wish," she scoffed. "What about Geek Girls?"

The charity his parents—his dad a neurosurgeon, his mom a cardiologist—had started. They'd seen how few opportunities there were for girls like their math-and-science-obsessed daughter, so they'd taken matters into their own hands, connecting girls interested in careers in science, technology, engineering, and math with mentors in their chosen fields, creating programs that taught girls how to write code, and publishing an online magazine with a different STEM theme each month.

The charity had struggled in the lean years after the accident, but one of the first things Eli had done when he made it big was get Geek Girls back on its feet. For his parents. And for Paige. "What about it?"

"The silent auction's the second Saturday in April. Will you be there?"

Eli sat up, eyes open. "Of course I will. You know I wouldn't miss that for the world."

"Even if you're still hibernating in Brooklyn?"

"For you and Geek Girls, I'll come out of my cave." Even if that meant he'd have to deal with Simon, who served with Eli and his sister on the board of directors and was bound to be in attendance as well.

"I take it back. You're not an arrogant jerk. You're a prince among men."

Great, he thought as they said their good-byes and he hung up the phone. Now if only he could get Brooke to agree.

Chapter Five

"Damn it, damn it, damn it, damn it."

Brooke turned off the tap and frantically grabbed for a dishtowel, trying to stem the flood of water flowing from the pipe beneath her kitchen sink. The same pipe she'd fixed with plumber's putty not three weeks ago.

Not having a super was turning into a serious pain in the ass. She'd briefly considered tucking her tail between her legs and running home to her family's Long Island estate. Emphasis on "briefly." But even twenty-four rooms weren't enough for her and her father to avoid each other.

She did her best to mop up the mess, then stuck her head under the sink to survey the damage. Plumber's putty wasn't going to cut it this time. The ancient copper pipe looked like it had burst, a gouge at least an inch long splitting it open.

"Damn it," she repeated, backing out from under the sink and slumping to the floor. This was way beyond her limited home repair abilities. She'd have to call a professional, which meant forking over money she didn't have and wasn't willing to beg her parents for.

Her cell rang, and she scrambled across the room on all fours to answer it. Her finger hovered over the screen when she saw her mother's name. Pamela Sinclair Worthington was the last person in the world she wanted to talk to right now. But if she ignored the call, it would be ten times worse later.

"Hey, Mom." Brooke flopped onto the couch, stretching out her legs in front of her. Her bare toes were in dire need of a pedicure, and if she rolled up her yoga pants, her legs were long overdue for a shave. Two things she tended to neglect in winter. It wasn't like she had anyone to impress. "What's up?"

"You tell me." The censure in her mother's voice washed over her like an ice bath, and Brooke was glad they weren't on FaceTime. Her flyaway hair, grease-smudged face, and stained Cowboy Bebop T-shirt would ramp up her mother's disapproval by a factor of a thousand. Maybe more. "You never call."

Wonder why that is?

"I've been busy," Brooke lied. Sure, her schedule was jam-packed. But she could have made time for a quick phone call. If she wanted to subject herself to scorn and derision, which she didn't. "My agent has me making changes to the book so we can…"

"Still working on your little comic book?" her mother asked, cutting her off. "How long has it been? Two years?"

Two and a half. And Brooke had several others in various stages of completion, too. Not that her mother cared. "It's a graphic novel, Mom. And yes, it's the one I've been trying to get published."

"Have you considered the possibility that it's not worthy of publication?"

"My agent thinks it is." *Even if you and Dad don't.*

"Then why is she making you change it?"

"That's how edits work."

"You know, I read somewhere that most authors make

less than ten thousand dollars a year."

"I'm well aware of that." Brooke rubbed the back of her neck. "That's why I tend bar. And freelance."

More of the latter, lately, than the former. An ad agency she'd done some work for had started throwing clients her way, allowing her to cut back her hours at the bar. She was still at Flotsam and Jetsam two or three times a week. But freelancing was way more lucrative, especially in the dead of winter. And it meant she was using her expensive bachelor of fine arts degree for more than "scribbling on napkins," as her father put it.

"Hardly respectable. Or stable." Her mother let out a sigh that reverberated across the phone line and could probably be heard throughout Nassau County. "You know you're welcome to work in the marketing department at Worthington Resorts International. I'm sure they'd be happy to have you."

"I'll keep that in mind." *Not.* Working for her family's hotel chain might be all right for her younger sister, who didn't have an adventurous bone in her fragile body, but Brooke was more of a free spirit. She couldn't handle being stuck in an office all day. "Was there a reason for this call?"

Other than to make me feel like shit on the bottom of your Louboutins?

"Your father wanted me to remind you about brunch on the fifth."

"He couldn't call himself?"

"You know him. All work, all the time."

She did, and he certainly was. It was how he'd built an empire—and alienated his eldest daughter. "I'll be there."

Like she was there the first Sunday of every month. Although she'd rather listen to Kim Kardashian read *War and Peace.*

"Heirloom. Eleven sharp."

Because it had to be a five-star restaurant. No simple

gathering around the kitchen table for the Worthingtons. "Got it."

"Mallory's bringing her beau. She'd like you to meet him."

Brooke gritted her teeth. "I said I'd be there."

"Very well. Feel free to bring a date of your own, if you're seeing anyone."

Right. Like she'd subject anyone to that hell on earth. "I'm not."

"Of course," her mother said, sounding like she'd smelled something especially vile. "And Brooke?"

"Yes?" She clutched a throw pillow to her chest with her free hand, bracing herself. From the arch tone of her mother's voice, whatever was coming next was sure to cut like a surgical laser.

"Wear something nice, not those rags you call a wardrobe. And nothing too low cut. Borrow something from your sister if you have to. You should be able to squeeze into one of her Oscar de la Rentas."

Luckily for her mother, Brooke ended the call without bothering to respond. What did you say when your own mother called you a slob, a slut, and a sow, all in one breath?

Brooke threw herself prostrate onto the couch, tossing the phone to the floor and burying her face in the pillow. First the sink. Now her mother. It was too much for one day.

"Why me?" she moaned into the stiff brocade. "What did I do to piss off the universe?"

"Anything I can do to help?"

She turned her head ever so slightly and cracked one eye open to find Eli standing in her doorway. As always, he looked like he'd stepped from the pages of a magazine. This time it was *Men's Health*, with butt-hugging jeans and a long-sleeved Henley that molded his sculpted torso. A stark contrast to her uncombed hair, grimy face, and soiled T-shirt. She retreated into the pillow.

Man, oh man. She must have really pissed off the universe.

"Everything okay?" he prodded.

"Have you heard the expression bad things come in threes?" she asked, her voice muffled by the pillow.

He chuckled. "Yeah."

"Well, you're number three."

"I'm bad?"

For my equilibrium.

"I keep you off balance?"

Damn. She wasn't supposed to say that out loud.

"Interesting."

"What are you doing here, anyway?" He'd been suspiciously out of sight since he'd last appeared at her door bearing a caffeinated peace offering eight days, six hours, thirty-two minutes, and seventeen seconds ago. Not that she was counting. She risked another glance at him. Big mistake. There were those dimples again, courtesy of that cocky, I-know-you-want-me smile. And how did he manage to have the perfect amount of sexy stubble morning, noon, and night? It was criminally unfair for one man to be so damned attractive.

"I knocked, but your door was open. As usual." He leaned a shoulder against the doorframe and crossed his arms. "What are numbers one and two?"

She blinked, both blinded by his hotness and confused by his question. Staring at him too long was like staring into the sun. You had to look away or get burned. "Huh?"

"You said I was the third bad thing to happen to you today. What are the first two?"

"The pipe under my sink is busted, and my mother thinks I'm an oversize tramp who doesn't know how to dress and can't hold down a decent job," she blurted before she could stop herself.

He didn't pry, letting it slide with an almost imperceptible lift of his eyebrow. "I'm no good with mothers, but pipes I can handle. Want me to take a look?"

No. "Sure. Thanks."

He strode over to her tiny kitchen like a man on a mission, a citrusy wave of his cologne teasing her nostrils as he passed by. He squatted in front of the open cabinet under the sink and pushed up his shirtsleeves, revealing sinewy forearms with a smattering of dark hair.

Brooke's heart lurched, and she had to remind herself to breathe. *Holy hell.* Since when had she found a man's forearms provocative?

Since about three seconds ago, apparently.

She took a few steps toward him, not wanting to get too close and risk falling under his sexy spell. "How much is this going to cost me?"

"Let me take a closer look."

He lay on his back and stuck his head under the sink. After a few seconds, he raised his arms to adjust something, exposing a strip of firm, bare flesh between the hem of his shirt and his waistband. The strip widened as he reached father up to tinker with a section of pipe closer to the drain. She took advantage of the opportunity to gawk unobserved, letting her eyes feast on his rock-hard abs—abs her naughty fingers remembered all too well and itched to get reacquainted with.

"You need a new U-bend." He scooted out from under the sink and stood, wiping his hands on his jeans.

She hastily averted her eyes, not wanting to get caught staring. "What's a U-bend?"

"The pipe that's shaped like a U. And while you're at it, I recommend PVC instead of copper. It's more efficient and durable, and it won't rust or burst. Parts shouldn't run more than thirty bucks. I can run to the hardware store and have them installed in a few hours."

"Oh, no. I wasn't asking you to..."

"You're right. You weren't asking. I was offering."

She bit her lip. Accepting help wasn't her forte. But she was stuck between a rock and a soggy place. "Are you sure it's not too much trouble?"

"Piece of cake." He jammed his thumbs in his pockets and rocked on his heels. "I've flipped a house or two in my day."

She eyed him suspiciously. He might look the part, but she hadn't forgotten the designer duds and high-end haircut he'd been sporting the night they met. "You don't seem like a manual labor kind of guy."

"You'd be surprised what kind of guy I am." The damn dimples were back, making her heart flutter. "So how about it? Am I hired?"

"Only if you let me pay you," she insisted, pressing her mouth into a thin, uncompromising line.

He considered it for a minute. "How about you feed me when I'm done? I like spaghetti."

Dinner? At her place? Just the two of them? Money would be a whole lot easier. And a lot less…tempting.

"Couldn't I give you cash?"

He shook his head. "Money I've got. Home cooking I don't."

"Fine." She couldn't screw up pasta too badly, could she? "But you'll probably wish my sister was at the stove. She's the chef."

"I doubt it." His eyes raked her up and down then flicked to his watch. "I'll be back in forty-five minutes."

She calculated how much time it would take her to shower and shave her legs. For her own benefit, of course. Not Eli's. A girl was entitled to feel good about herself, wasn't she? That was the only reason she was contemplating wearing the sheer lavender bra and panties at the back of her underwear drawer, tags still attached.

Liar.

"Can you make it an hour?" She shifted to hide a stain on her shirt. Pointless, she knew, as there were at least three more she couldn't conceal.

"Deal."

With a wink, he turned to leave, giving her a parting view of his fine, firm ass in those tight jeans before he disappeared out the door.

• • •

It was more like an hour and a half by the time Eli found himself back outside Brooke's apartment. He balanced his toolbox and the bags he'd gotten at Home Depot in his arms and knocked.

"Come in." Brooke's voice wafted through the door, along with the sweet smell of garlic and tomatoes. "It's open."

He grinned as he turned the knob and crossed the threshold. "Of course it is."

She stood in front of the stove with her back to him, stirring a large pot of what he deduced was spaghetti sauce and sneaking glances at a tablet propped up on the tiny square of countertop next to her. Gone were the yoga pants and stained T-shirt. In their place was a gray turtleneck sweater dress that followed her curves like a Formula 1 racer. A pair of black suede thigh-high boots completed the ensemble. He couldn't see her face, but her hair was gathered into a sexy, messy mass on top of her head.

He whistled. "You clean up nice."

"Thanks." Over her shoulder, she shot him a smile that lit up her face and sucker punched him in the gut. It wasn't only her hair and clothes she'd taken the time to fix. He didn't know much about makeup, but whatever she'd done to her face had the effect of bringing out the gold flecks in her eyes and making her already full lips look fuller. "I wish I could say the same about you, but you're going to get pretty dirty under there."

She jerked her head toward the sink. He put down the toolbox and bags and bent to open the cabinet. "I like getting dirty."

He thought he heard her mutter "don't I know it" before he flipped onto his back and poked his head under the sink to reassess the damage. "Can you hand me the pliers from my toolbox? And I'll need a pot or bucket to catch the water when I take this thing apart."

"Sure. Let me turn down the sauce."

"It smells great."

"Thanks. Did you know pasta was invented by the Chinese, and people ate it for thousands of years before anyone thought to add tomato sauce?"

His lips twitched. She was a babbler. Good sign. That meant she was nervous around him, and she wouldn't be nervous if she wasn't interested. "I had no idea."

She knelt beside him, giving him a tantalizing glimpse of creamy thigh over the top of her boots. He willed his dick to stand down and focused on the delicate hand holding out a wrench to him. Their fingers brushed as he took it and then the stockpot she offered, and for a second time in as many minutes he fought to control his raging hormones.

"I've got to take care of dinner," she said, the rasp in her voice telling him she wasn't unaffected, either. "Will you be okay without my help?"

"I'll be fine." A little space was probably a good thing. Much more of this and her pipe would stay broken and they'd never get to the food. "Go."

Unlike his new furniture, with its incomprehensible instructions, this job was straightforward, and he was able to replace the pipe in less than an hour, even with Brooke bustling around the kitchen, distracting him with her fresh, fruity scent, off-key humming, and occasional chitchat.

"All done," he called, his head and torso still in the cupboard. "Turn on the tap and let her rip."

"You might want to get out of there first," she suggested.

He let out a derisive snort. "Don't trust my handiwork?"

"It's your funeral."

He heard her fiddle with the faucet, and the water started flowing.

"Dry as the Sahara." He slid out from under the sink and sat up. "Mission accomplished."

"Thanks again." She blushed and turned her attention back to the pot of sauce simmering on the stove, and he got the feeling accepting help didn't come easily to her. "Dinner will be ready in about ten minutes if you want to wash up. I put out a fresh washcloth and towel for you in the bathroom."

"Sounds good." He put his tools back in the box and swept the mess he'd made into one of the empty Home Depot bags. "Where's your garbage?"

She inclined her head toward a stainless-steel trash can next to the refrigerator. He tossed the bag inside and headed for the bathroom. When he emerged a few minutes later, hands scrubbed and nails as free from grease as he could get them, Brooke was setting the cafe table that served as her dinette set.

Eli smoothed down his rumpled Henley the best he could and crossed over to her. "Anything I can do?"

"You can open a bottle of wine." She held up two bottles. "I've got red and white. Pick your poison."

"Red." He took the bottle of cabernet sauvignon she offered, making sure their fingers didn't make contact this time so he wouldn't be tempted to clear off the table she'd set and take her right then and there. "Where's your corkscrew?"

"Top drawer next to the sink."

He squeezed past her to get the bottle opener, struck by the intimacy of it all. And not because they were jockeying for position in her tiny galley kitchen. It was more how, despite their close confines, they worked together with an easy familiarity, like an old married couple.

The thought should've terrified him. It didn't.

Weird.

"Find it?" she asked, snapping him out of his reverie.

"Got it." He hip-checked the drawer closed.

"Glasses are on the counter."

He opened the bottle, poured them each a glass, and handed one to Brooke, who was back at the stove. She took a sip and set it down on the counter beside her.

"Sit. I'll fix our plates and bring them over."

"I could…"

"Sit," she repeated, pointing a slender finger at the cafe table. "Relax. I'm supposed to be paying you back for fixing my sink."

He obeyed, sipping his wine while she ladled out spaghetti and sauce onto two plates and brought them to the table. She sat opposite him and crossed her legs in those come-fuck-me boots, the movement inching her dress higher up on her thighs.

The next hour was a mix of pain and pleasure. Pain because sitting across from Brooke, watching the unconsciously erotic way she slurped her spaghetti, was torture of the highest degree. Pleasure because when he could concentrate on something other than her long legs and luscious lips, he found he really enjoyed talking with her.

They kept the conversation light, avoiding hot-button topics like politics or religion. By the time they finished eating and he'd helped her clear their plates, he knew her favorite color (turquoise), where she went to college (Rhode Island School of Design), and the name of her first pet (a guinea pig she called Charcoal), among other things.

They were as compatible out of bed—or futon, if you wanted to get technical—as they were in it. They both had younger sisters who they tended to overprotect. His parents were gone. Her relationship with hers was strained, although she didn't say why and he didn't want to press her. And they had a mutual appreciation for Thai food, second British invasion bands, and reruns of *How I Met Your Mother*.

"I'm sorry," Brooke said when the last dish was dried and put away. "I don't have anything for dessert."

"I beg to differ." He came up behind her.

"No, seriously." She turned to face him, her mossy eyes bright with the desire he knew her lips were going to deny. "The only thing in my refrigerator that remotely resembles dessert is a can of Reddi-wip left over from Mr. Feingold's seventy-fifth birthday party."

"That wasn't exactly what I had in mind." He moved in again, resting one hand on her waist and cupping her cheek with the other. "Although it might come in handy."

She shook off the hand on her face, freeing several strands of hair from her sexily mussed updo. "We agreed. One night."

"Did we?" He brushed one long lock behind her ear. "I don't remember signing anything."

"It was an unspoken agreement."

"An agreement requires an offer and acceptance. And I refuse to accept your not-so-generous offer."

"What are you, a lawyer or something?"

"Just a guy who knows his way around a contract." The hand still on her hip tightened ever so slightly. "Tell you what. I'll make you a counteroffer."

"A counteroffer?"

An endearing wrinkle creased her forehead. He resisted the urge to kiss it away. How a woman could be adorable and alluring at the same time was beyond him, but the combination was turning out to be his Kryptonite.

"A repeat performance. And if it's not to your satisfaction…" He dropped his voice to a deliberately seductive purr on the last word, not above playing on the double entendre. "I'll walk away. No questions asked."

She pulled back as much as she could with the counter behind her and let out a long, regretful breath that hovered between them. For a moment, he thought he'd lost the battle, and he steeled himself to admit defeat. Then she lifted her chin, squared her shoulders, and met his heated gaze.

"Challenge accepted."

Chapter Six

Eli didn't waste any time, swooping in the second Brooke agreed to his ridiculous, risqué proposal and claiming her mouth. She was as needy and greedy, digging her fingers into the soft cotton of his Henley and pulling him forward.

Her brain might be able to list a hundred reasons why this was wrong. But all her body knew was that it felt oh so right.

With her surrender complete, Eli took full advantage, coaxing her lips apart and sweeping the inside of her mouth with his tongue. He slipped one hand into her hair, undoing her artfully messy topknot and gently tugging her head back so he could deepen their kiss. The other one slid under her knee and lifted her leg, wrapping it around his hip.

"I do have a bed," she panted when he finally released her mouth to trace a hot, wet trail along her jaw to her ear.

"We'll get there." He nipped the lobe, making her gasp. "Eventually."

The gasp morphed into a full-out moan as he drew the sensitive skin behind her ear into his mouth. "It's always hurry up and wait with you."

"More like slow down and enjoy the scenery."

He pulled back to study her, his normally bright eyes dark and heavy-lidded. The sudden loss of his lips on her skin made her desperate with desire, burning from the inside out.

"So I'm the scenery?" she asked.

He nodded. His eyes flicked from her free-flowing hair to her breasts, nipples straining against her knit dress, past her hips, down her legs in her thigh-hugging boots, then back again. "And the scenery's wearing far too much clothing."

The inferno inside her flared hotter. "You don't say."

"I do." He slid his hands down her body and reached for the hem of her dress, inching it up her thighs. "I prefer the raw, unspoiled beauty of nature."

She lifted her arms over her head, letting him peel off the offending garment. He dropped it to the floor, and she stood before him in her boots, bra, and panties. She bent to unzip one of the boots, but he put a hand on her shoulder, stopping her.

"Keep them on," he rumbled in her ear. "I've been fantasizing about fucking you in those boots from the second I walked in the door."

"Really?" She rose slowly until her punch-drunk gaze met his. "No wonder it took you so long to fix the sink."

"Did not." He snaked a hand around her back and skillfully released the clasp of her bra.

She dropped her shoulders. The straps slithered down her arms, and the scrap of lavender lace and silk landed at her feet, leaving her bare breasts on display. "Did, too."

"Not." He closed his fingers around the waistband of her panties and dragged them down her legs, over the boots.

She lifted one foot, then the other, stepping out of her underwear and kicking them to the side. "Too."

Eli hoisted her up onto the counter and spread her legs, fitting himself between them and silencing her with another hard, fast kiss. "Enough talk. Time for some action."

Brooke held up a hand. "Not so fast, hotshot."

He took a slight step back, his face a frustrated mix of lust and confusion. "Now who's trying to slow things down?"

"One of us is still overdressed." She waved a hand up and down his fine but fully clothed form.

"That's easily remedied."

He whipped off his Henley, treating her to an eyeful of rippling pecs and washboard abs, kicked off his shoes, and went to work on his jeans. She almost told him to stop so she could finish the job herself, but she was too eager to see him, to touch him, to have his mouth back on hers and his hands on her breasts, teasing her aching nipples into points.

"There," he said when he was fully, gloriously naked and had reclaimed his rightful place between her legs. "Satisfied?"

"I will be." Her eyes strayed to his already impressive erection, standing stiff and proud against his flat stomach, and she licked her lips. Satisfied was putting it mildly. She willed her gaze back to his face. "You promised, remember? Or you'll walk away without any questions."

He flashed her his trademark cocky, panty-melting grin, obviously amused and flattered by her unabashed ogling. "Then I'd better deliver. Because I don't have any intention of walking away from you anytime soon."

Within seconds, his mouth was on her again. This time, he bypassed her lips for the tender flesh of her breast, his tongue sliding warm and wet over the creamy mound to her nipple. She cried out and arched into him, grabbing on to his broad shoulders for support. He rewarded her with a scrape of his teeth before sucking her nipple into his mouth.

She clawed at his upper arms, her fingernails marking his skin as she writhed against him. It was good, so damn good, but she wanted—needed—more.

"More, huh?" He smiled against her damp skin. Her

inner monologue had escaped again, but she didn't mind one damn bit, not if it meant he'd give her what she was asking for. Wasn't that the point of all those *Cosmo* articles about how to communicate in bed? "Like this?"

His hand ghosted over her abdomen until he cupped her sex. One long finger slipped between her folds, brushing her swollen clit. She gasped and pulled one knee up to her chest, planting her boot flat on the countertop and giving him an all-access pass to her privates.

"Still not enough?" he taunted, wagging a brow at her blatant invitation. "How about this?"

Without warning, he dropped to his knees and buried his head between her legs. His tongue teased her with slow, agonizing circles, avoiding the spot where she needed him most.

Brooke moaned and let her legs fall farther apart. Her entire world had narrowed to his mouth and the magic it was working on her body. She closed her eyes, and her head dropped back, smacking the cabinet behind her. Her eyes flew open, and her mouth twisted into a grimace. "Ouch."

Eli raised his head. "Are you…?"

She fisted her hands in his hair and pulled him back to her, silencing him. "I'm fine. Better than fine. Don't you dare stop."

He smiled against her as she squirmed to meet his elusive tongue. "Wouldn't dream of it."

He resumed his onslaught with renewed vigor. God, how she'd missed this. Not the subtle scrape of tongue against flesh, the gentle suction of lips on her. Okay, so she'd missed that. A lot. But more she'd missed the closeness, the intimacy that came with sex. At least with good sex. And this was better than good sex. It was mind-altering, body-tingling, soul-melting sex.

In less time than she wanted to admit, Eli had her

tumbling over the edge into oblivion. He stayed with her as she bucked and writhed with pleasure. Only when the last tremor had subsided did he release her and look up her body. The cocky grin was back.

"Mission accomplished. You look damn good and satisfied to me."

"I can't argue with that." She glanced down at his erection, still stiff and ready for action. "But what about you?"

"Don't worry about me." He rose slowly and found his jeans on the floor behind him. Her heart sank and she grabbed the lip of the counter in a white-knuckle grip. Was that it? Had he won their little bet to prove a point, and now he was walking away?

Then he pulled out his wallet, took out a condom, and tore it open. With swift, sure moves he sheathed himself. Her girly bits sprang to life again at the sight of his smooth, strong fingers rolling the rubber down his shaft. They tingled faster when he stepped back between her waiting thighs and ran a hand along the soft suede of one of her boots. "My fantasy is about to come true. Having you beneath me in nothing but these sinfully sexy shoes."

• • •

Eli had always prided himself on being in control at all times. Whether it was in the boardroom or the bedroom, he never let his emotions get the best of him.

Until Brooke.

That night at the bar, he hadn't been able to resist her. And it had been hell on earth sleeping a few feet down the hall from her without banging down her door and screwing her senseless. Now that he had her spread out in front of him in those infernal boots, her hair in loose, wild waves about her face, her eyes wide, and her plump lips slightly parted and begging to be kissed, the odds of him staying cool and in command were about as good as his chance of buying Central Park from the city of New York and turning it into a parking lot.

He guided his cock to her entrance, rubbing the tip through her wet heat. One thrust and he'd be inside her, enveloped in all that delicious warmth. Holding back was torture, pure and simple. "Tell me you're ready for this."

"I am." She lifted her hips to meet him, as if to prove her point. "Please."

That was all the encouragement he needed. He entered her, hard and fast, no pretense of gentleness. There would be time for sweet and slow later. This was the time for hot-and-heavy, wall-banging, piss-off-the-neighbors sex. Which was fine, because Charise was spending a couple of days with her baby daddy's family in New Jersey, and he was Brooke's next closest neighbor.

And he certainly wasn't complaining.

"Fuck." He ground the word out through clenched teeth and started to move. Sweat beaded on his forehead as he pushed in as far as he could, filling her completely.

She let out a sharp hiss of breath but stayed with him all the way, her arms coming up to loop around his neck. He grabbed the edge of the counter on either side of her shapely hips and pounded into her, his thrusts growing faster, wilder with each encouraging moan from her lips.

"I can't wait much longer," he said between heavy breaths.

"Don't," she coaxed him, her husky voice dripping with lust, almost finishing him off. "Let go."

He closed his eyes and tried to think of absorption rates and environmental impact statements. "You first."

Her fingers tangled in his hair, and her mouth curved into a seductive smile that tugged at him, balls-deep. "I already crossed the finish line, remember?"

As if he could forget the sight of her coming apart beneath him, her head thrust back, eyes closed, mouth in a perfect, ecstatic "O." She wrecked him, this woman, in a way no other had. He didn't understand it, didn't know how or why she alone had awakened some primal, protective urge in him that was previously dormant. And to be honest, he didn't care. It felt right. It felt good.

He pressed his lips to the soft skin between her breasts, taking a light nip to sample her sweetness before lifting his head. "I was hoping I could get you across it again."

"Oh, you will." She gazed up at him in a way that made both his chest and his cock swell. "We've got all night, right?"

"Damn right."

He drove into her again and again until he shuddered and exploded with an almost guttural groan. When his breathing evened, he brushed a damp hair off her cheek and rested his forehead on hers. "That was…"

"Yeah." The word came out on a sigh that tickled the underside of his jaw.

"I'm not usually so…"

"Passionate?" she finished for him. "Forceful?"

"Fast." He scrubbed a hand through his sweat-slicked hair. "Rough."

She pressed a kiss to the still racing pulse at his throat. "I like fast and rough."

"I hope you like slow and gentle, too. Because that's where we're headed next."

He carefully withdrew and disposed of the condom in the trash can. Then he scooped her up and carried her out of the kitchen.

She wrapped her legs around his waist and held on to his shoulders, her fingernails digging little crescents into his skin. With each step he took, her suede boots rubbed seductively against his hips and ass. "Where to?"

"I think it's about time we found ourselves a bed, don't you?"

"No objections from this corner."

Her makeshift bedroom was at the opposite end of the studio, behind a folding screen that gave her some privacy. He deposited her onto the plush, dove-gray comforter and followed her down, stretching out beside her. As promised, he took his time with her this go-round, worshiping her body with his hands and mouth. He couldn't get enough of the feel or the taste of her. It didn't take anything more than a simple look or the barest touch to turn him into a starving man at an all-you-can-eat buffet. She must have felt the same hunger because she returned the favor, exploring him from every angle until they were both finally sated and spent.

They lay tangled together in a sex-drugged haze. No recriminations. No regrets. No awkward post-coital conversation. Just two people who had scratched a mutual itch they couldn't ignore.

At least, that's what Eli's brain tried to tell him as they drifted to sleep, even as his heart told him it was fast moving into something more. Something new and unfamiliar that he hadn't known existed.

When he awoke, the other side of the bed was empty. Sunlight spilled in from the double-hung window, and the smell of freshly brewed coffee teased his nostrils.

Holy hell. He'd stayed the night. It usually took him months to get to that point with a woman. But not Brooke. His first time alone with her in her apartment—hell, his first time in her bed—and he hadn't wanted to leave this smart, strong, sensual woman who made him chuckle one minute and climax the next.

He didn't have time to overanalyze the situation, thank fuck, because the woman in question appeared beside him, a steaming mug in her hand. She looked sixty shades of sexy, her eyes still misty with sleep and her hair all morning-mussed and flowing freely around her shoulders. She'd thrown on a tank top and a pair of form-fitting workout pants that didn't leave much to the imagination—not that he needed to imagine the curves and valleys he'd spent hours memorizing last night—and he adjusted the sheet to hide the beginning of yet another raging, Brooke-induced hard-on.

"I wasn't sure how you took your morning caffeine, but you strike me as a strong and dark kind of guy." She bent to set the mug on the bedside table, giving him an eyeful of her magnificent cleavage.

He sat up, letting the covers fall to his waist, and her gaze lighted on his bare chest. Her breathing quickened, and her tongue darted out to wet her lips, making his already erect cock impossibly harder. She was as ready for round three as he was. Or was it four? He'd lost count somewhere during the night.

Eli reached for the mug and took a sip of hot coffee. "Perfect."

"I'm not much of a breakfast person, but I've got a box of peanut butter Captain Crunch in the cabinet if you're hungry. It's like crack to me. Or if you'd prefer something more sophisticated, I can whip up some french toast."

He was hungry. But not for Captain Crunch or french toast. What he was craving would take more than the—he glanced at the digital clock on the nightstand—fifteen minutes he had before his telephone status conference with Ginny. Hopefully she had a lead on their mole and some news about his bid for Candy Court.

The second thought sobered him for a moment, but he shook it off. He'd already started preliminary discussions with a couple of local landlords who had space available. If the sale went through, all of the tenants, including Brooke, would have suitable substitute housing in Sunset Park before one brick was disturbed at Candy Court. No, not suitable. Better. Together, because they'd formed a sort of family he didn't want to split up. More affordable. In a neighborhood revitalized by the new and improved Candy Court. It was the perfect solution for everyone involved, not just him.

"Thanks, but as much as I'd like to stay, I'll have to pass on breakfast. I've got an early status conference." He looked around for his clothes then realized they were probably still where he'd shed them—in the kitchen, on the other side of the privacy screen.

"Status conference?" Brooke picked up a pile from a nearby chair and handed him his neatly folded shirt, jeans, and boxer briefs. While he'd been dead to the world, she'd been busy playing housewife. Making him coffee. Folding his clothes. The casual domesticity was strangely satisfying, but her next words hit him like a splash of cold water, dousing his momentary contentment. "What exactly is it that you do for a living?"

Shit. Him and his big fucking mouth. He'd been so eager to assure her that he wasn't running out the door without good reason he hadn't considered that his reason might touch on secrets he wasn't ready to expose. Soon, but not yet. And certainly not when he was about to head out the door after a night of mind-blowing, life-altering sex. This wasn't something he could blurt out and run. "I'm in finance."

It wasn't a lie. Exactly. He worked with numbers every day. Cap rates. Overruns. Closing costs.

His stomach roiled at the half-truth, but it would have to do. For now.

"Figures." She rolled her eyes.

"Right. Numbers." He shucked off the covers and slid on his boxers then his jeans.

"No, I mean it figures you're a financial guy. I had you pegged from the minute you walked into Flotsam and Jetsam."

"Really?" He slipped his shirt over his head and stuck his arms through the sleeves. "I didn't realize I was that transparent. What gave me away?"

"I think it was the designer duds. Or maybe the top-shelf scotch." She crossed her arms over her ample chest and squinted at him. "Which begs the question. What's a high-rent guy like you doing in a low-rent place like this?"

"Would you believe me if I said I like things low-rent?"

"No." She stared him down.

He was saved from further interrogation by the alarm on his cell phone. He pulled it out of his pocket and swiped the screen to silence it.

"Let me guess." She bent to pick up his shoes and handed them to him. "Time for you to wow Wall Street?"

"If you mean my status conference, then yes." He sat to slide on his sneakers, a beat-up pair of Converse Chuck Taylor All Stars Ginny had dug out from the back of his closet. Nothing high-rent about them.

"Well, it's been fun." Brooke flipped her hair back, trying too hard to seem casual. "I'll see you around, I guess."

He stood and took her by the shoulders. "Stop."

"Stop what?"

"Pretending this thing between us is over."

"Isn't it?"

"No." Not by a long shot. He wasn't giving up the best thing that had happened to him since he made his first million. And that paled in comparison to the feelings Brooke stirred in him, feelings he couldn't quite put into words. His alarm chimed again, and he silenced it. "It isn't."

He kissed her hard and fast to prove his point, like an exclamation mark on his declaration. "Are you working tonight?"

She blinked up at him. "No. I'm off until Thursday."

"Good. I'll pick you up at seven. Dress casual."

He kissed her again, only slightly gentler than the last time. Then, without another word, he crossed the room and strode out the door, knowing he'd left her in the same condition he was in. Hot, bothered, and wanting more.

Chapter Seven

Brooke read the tile sign on the station wall as the subway train slowed: GREENPOINT. "For the hundredth time, where are you taking me?"

Eli gave her the same secretive smile he'd given her every other time she'd asked the question on their forty-five-minute underground journey. "For the hundredth time, be patient and you'll find out."

"You're the newcomer. Shouldn't I be the one showing you around town?"

"You have." He stood as the train came to a stop, and she did the same. "You took me to that little Italian restaurant where the ninety-year-old owner still makes meatballs by hand every day. Introduced me to the joys of walking the Brooklyn Bridge in a snowstorm. Now it's my turn. They say you never take advantage of what's in your own backyard."

"A few flurries hardly amount to a snowstorm." She jockeyed for position next to him as they waited with a cluster of noisy teenagers for the doors to slide open. "And almost an hour on the subway's not exactly my own backyard."

"Close enough." He extended a gloved hand, and she took it with her own. Two layers of fleece and she could still feel the heat that erupted between them at even the most innocent touch. Not that there had been many of those. It seemed every time they got their hands on each other they wound up naked and horizontal. "Trust me, it'll be worth it."

"I'm sure it will." If there was one thing she'd learned in the weeks since Eli had fixed her plumbing—pun intended—it was that no time spent with him was wasted. He had a way of turning the most mundane things, like washing dishes or grocery shopping, into special occasions.

Or maybe it's not the occasion that's special, a voice in her head taunted. *Maybe it's the man.*

She ignored it, the commitment-phobe in her not ready for the feelings Eli was stirring up, and followed him up the stairs to the street. Their breath made little clouds in the crisp, clear evening air as they walked the few blocks to Manhattan Avenue, where Eli pulled up short in front of an unassuming storefront. The sign above the door identified it as the Sunshine Laundromat and Cleaners. Someone inside obviously had a sense of humor because another sign in the window read: "Try our gourmet vegetarian washing machines and vegan dryers."

"Here we are," Eli announced, sounding as proud as if he'd won Olympic gold or ended global warming.

"There must be a hundred Laundromats between here and Sunset Park," Brooke observed. "And it's going to be hard to wash our clothes when they're back at home."

"Who said anything about washing clothes?"

"What else is there to do at a Laundromat? Watch strangers' unmentionables get tossed around in the dryer?" She tightened her scarf around her neck and blew into her gloves. Damn, it was cold. Spring couldn't get there soon enough. Brooklyn came alive when the weather warmed up.

Hunting for bargains at the Brooklyn Flea Market. Playing bocce in Brooklyn Bridge Park. Feeding the goats at the Prospect Park Zoo.

Maybe some people didn't take advantage of what was happening in their own neighborhood, but not Brooke. She loved the quirky, offbeat vibe of the borough she'd chosen to make her home. And so did Eli, clearly. She could picture them in summer, watching the sun set over Manhattan from—

No, no, no, no, no. She wasn't doing that. She wasn't thinking past today. This was about the here and the now and nothing more.

"Cold?" Eli put his arm around her, drawing her tight. "Let's go inside. I promise you won't be disappointed."

"By a Laundromat?" She burrowed into him. The guy radiated heat like a furnace. Sleeping next to him was like spooning with the sun. "You've seen the huge pile of dirty clothes in my closet, right? Doing laundry isn't my jam."

"I told you, we're not doing laundry. And this isn't your typical Laundromat."

"What have they got in there?" She peered through the window but couldn't see much of anything. "Salsa dancers? A bowling alley?"

"No and no." He pulled the door open and gestured for her to lead the way inside. "But I'll add those to my list of possible future outings."

He had a list of possible future outings? Her heart stuttered, but her inner commitment-phobe stepped in again and tamped it down.

Here and now. Nothing more.

She obeyed his unspoken request and crossed the threshold. At first glance, nothing seemed out of the ordinary. A row of washing machines on one wall, dryers against the other. Those metal carts for transferring laundry. Tables for folding. A couple of late-night customers sat in uncomfortable-looking plastic chairs watching the Rangers game on a flat-screen TV. The only things out of place were two ancient pinball machines in the corner.

"Pinball?" She eyed the machines, which looked like they'd seen better days. "Do those things even work?"

"Sure do. But that's nothing." He followed her inside, letting the door close behind them, and led her past the lines of washers and dryers to the back of the building. "Wait until you see what's behind here."

He stood in front of what looked like two driers built into the wall, one on top of the other.

She raised a questioning eyebrow. "Behind where?"

"Here." He tapped the top dryer. "Push."

She did. A hidden door swung open, and she stepped through. What greeted her on the other side was a pinball lover's ultimate fantasy. Vintage machines with names like Medieval Madness, Attack from Mars, and Tales of the Arabian Nights ringed the room. At least half of the twenty-plus machines were in use, bells clanging and lights flashing as scores mounted. At the far end of the room, a bar served wine and beer.

"How did you find this place?"

"Yelp." He flashed her a crooked grin. "I thought we could try something a little different."

She grinned back. "It's different, all right."

He rubbed his chin, ruffling his four-day beard, and her fingers itched to follow suit. "Good different or bad different?"

"Definitely good. I haven't played pinball in ages." Before Mallory had gotten sick, they'd had a summer house in Wildwood, New Jersey. Rainy days meant hours spent in the arcade on the boardwalk. She'd held the record on Orbiter 1 for almost two seasons.

"Me, either. Thought it might be fun." He took a handful of coins out of his pocket and jangled them. "So, what do you say? Winner gets to pick the pizza toppings."

"I've got a better idea." She trailed a finger down his arm.

He shivered under her touch, and when he spoke, his voice was low and smoky. "Can't wait to hear it."

She rose up on tiptoe and brought her lips to his ear. "Winner gets to decide where and how we have sex tonight."

He grabbed her wandering hand and tugged her over to the nearest machine. "You're on like Donkey Kong."

• • •

If there was one thing Brooke hated more than Sunday brunch with her family… Strike that. There was nothing Brooke hated more than her parents' monthly excuse for putting her through the wringer. The only redeeming thing was her sister Mallory smiling at her from a table across the restaurant when Brooke entered.

"Hey, Mal." She crossed the room and greeted her sister with a warm hug. Was it her imagination, or did Mallory seem thinner, more frail than usual? Brooke gave her one more squeeze before releasing her and taking a seat at the otherwise empty table. "Where are the 'rents?"

Mallory sat next to her. "On their way. They hit traffic on the Cross Island Expressway."

"Good. That gives us some time to catch up." Brooke motioned for a waiter. She was going to need a mimosa to get through this meal with her self-esteem intact. Or a bloody mary. Or both.

Her sister blushed. "Until Hunter gets back. He's in the lobby, answering a call. You probably walked right by him."

"The doctor you've been seeing?"

Mallory nodded.

Brooke screwed up her forehead in concentration, trying to picture who she'd rushed past in her hurry to find her family.

Heaven forbid she show up late and give her parents—her mother, especially—more ammunition to attack her with. Like they needed help in that department.

Brooke gave herself a mental smack upside the head and focused on remembering who she'd seen on her way into the restaurant. After a few seconds, she snapped her fingers. "Got it. Dirty-blond hair, charcoal suit, cell phone glued to his ear?"

Mallory bristled. "Hunter is a highly respected oncologist. Tops in his field. And he's on call this weekend. People are depending on him."

"Relax, Mal. I'm not criticizing him." Yet. Brooke would reserve judgment. Although the fact that their parents had given Hunter their seal of approval was already a huge-ass strike against him. "Just describing him."

"Sorry." Mallory gave Brooke a wan smile and smoothed the skirt of her gray silk Yves St. Laurent sheath dress, which she'd paired with a strand of pearls, matching earrings, and black patent leather pumps. She exuded class, style, and sophistication, a stark contrast to Brooke's retro burgundy dress, beige cardigan, cable knit tights, and brown leather ankle boots. "I really want you to like him."

"It's not me that has to like him, it's you." Brooke gave her sister a playful poke. "Besides, you already know my opinion on this subject. No man's good enough for my baby sister."

The waiter came by, and they ordered their drinks—the aforementioned bloody mary for Brooke and an orange juice for Mallory.

"No alcohol?" Brooke asked when he was gone. "Is there something you want to tell me?"

"I'm not pregnant, if that's what you're hinting at." Mallory unfolded her napkin and placed it in her lap. "Hunter doesn't approve of drinking in the middle of the day."

Strike two against Hunter, and Brooke hadn't even met him yet. "That's all well and good for him, but there's no way I'll make it through an entire meal with Mom and Dad without a little liquid courage."

"Come on, they're not that bad."

"To you." Their perfect, miracle child. The one who survived cancer and graduated top of her class at the Culinary Institute of America. The one working her way up the ranks in the kitchen of the Fifth Avenue Worthington, the family chain's flagship hotel.

Not that Brooke resented her sister. Each and every one of the choices Mallory had made—from culinary school to working in the family business—were ones that were right for her. Brooke wished their parents could see that she had done the same thing, that they had two very different daughters, and that the life she'd chosen, while not the one they wanted her to have, was right for her.

"They only want you to be happy," Mallory insisted.

"Yeah, so long as my definition of happy matches theirs."

Mallory shook her head and took a sip from her water glass. Brooke followed suit. The cool water did nothing to douse her rising irritation. She should be used to it by now, but her parents' seeming inability to remotely understand her still had the ability to piss her off if she let it. She took a deep breath and released it, long and slow. With each puff of air, she felt her anger dissipate, downshifting her mood from royally ticked to mildly miffed.

"I'm sorry, Mal." Brooke reached across the table and squeezed her sister's hand. "I promise I'll be on my best behavior for your doctor."

"Your best behavior?" Mallory laughed and squeezed back. "That's not saying much."

The waiter delivered their drinks. Brooke had barely taken a sip of her bloody mary when their parents showed up with Mallory's doctor in tow. Introductions were made and more drinks ordered—coffee and juice, straight up. No alcohol before noon for the perfect people.

"So, Brooke," her mother started in once the waiter left to fetch their beverages of choice. "No one joining you today?"

Brooke risked a glance at the cell phone to the right of her place setting, where she'd strategically placed it in the hope that it would ring so she could feign some sort of emergency and escape. Under ten minutes from arrival to insult. A record, even for her mother.

"Obviously," she said, gesturing to the empty chair beside her.

"Hunter." Her mother turned her attention to Mallory's beau, and for a moment Brooke thought she'd been spared, at least temporarily. "Surely you know some eligible men for Brooke. One of your colleagues at the clinic, perhaps. Or maybe a former classmate at Columbia."

"How about Felix Oliver?" her father suggested. "Don't you play tennis with him at the Vanderbilt Club?"

"I believe he's recently engaged." Hunter eyed Brooke, his mouth drawing into a thin, critical line. "But I'm sure I could dredge someone up."

Strike three.

She and Mallory were going to have a long talk when they were alone. Her gaze shifted to her sister, who fidgeted uncomfortably in her chair, her eyes downcast and her expression solemn. She needed to ditch this judgmental asshole and fast. What did she see in him, anyway? Okay, so he was supposedly some sort of rock star in the medical community. That didn't give him the right to be a pretentious prick.

"Thanks, but no thanks." Brooke took a healthy slug of her bloody mary and frowned. Not nearly strong enough to survive this shit storm. She said a silent prayer the waiter would hurry back so she could order another, sans tomato juice. "I can dredge up my own dates."

When she wanted to. And lately she certainly hadn't had any problem, thanks to a certain stubborn number cruncher who was supposed to have been a one-night stand. Emphasis on supposed to have been.

The guy was nothing if not persistent. Since their visit to the Laundromat-cum-arcade, he'd convinced her to visit the sea lions at the New York Aquarium, ride the East River Ferry, and tour the Brooklyn Navy Yard. God only knew what he had up his sleeve next.

And that was during daylight hours. Then there were the nights. Long, leisurely nights filled with every kind of sex a person could imagine, and some that hadn't entered her wildest dreams. And she'd had some pretty wild dreams. Slow, steamy shower sex. Hard and fast, up-against-the-wall sex. Half-clothed, bent-over-the-kitchen-counter sex. And one particularly memorable bout of semi-public sex in the back of a taxi on the way home from Brooke's favorite Indian restaurant, a little hole in the wall in Park Slope with the best chicken tikka masala east of the river.

Step-by-step, inch-by-inch, Eli had worn her down, stormed past her defenses and wormed his way into her daily—and nightly—routine. Which, while it had certain fringe benefits like multiple orgasms, also scared the ever-loving shit out of her. Because the truth was, orgasms or not, she was really starting to like the guy.

At first glance, he might have looked like every entitled asshole she went to high school with. But underneath his designer duds, Eli was about as different from those jerks as peanut butter was from jelly. Being with him was easy. No expectations. No pressure. She could dress how she wanted, do what she wanted, say what she wanted without worrying about being held up to some artificial standard of perfection. Instead of judging her, he listened—really listened like he was interested, like he cared about her thoughts and opinions.

Which presented Brooke with a ginormous problem. She did not—repeat, *did not*—do relationships. Yet with each passing day, with every new adventure in and out of the bedroom, what they were doing was starting to look more and more like just that. A—*gasp*—relationship. One that was already messing with her five-year plan. Hell, she'd barely written in the weeks since their infamous spaghetti dinner. Her pages sat on her drawing board, untouched, mocking her. Like the email from her agent asking how the revisions were coming along, which she hadn't responded to.

She had to get it together and fast. Compartmentalize things. Work in one neat and tidy box, hot sex—and nothing else—with Eli in another. It was that or end things with him all together, a thought that was strangely terrifying to her.

"That would be lovely, Hunter," her mother blithely continued as if Brooke hadn't shot down her little matchmaking scheme. It was hard to believe, looking at her now, but Pamela Worthington had once been a promising opera singer, a mezzo-soprano the *Times* called "a vocal powerhouse." She'd left all that behind for the sake of her "perfect" society marriage, and she expected her daughters to do the same.

Fat chance, Brooke thought. Mallory might be willing to play along, but Brooke had her own ideas about her future. And none of them included sacrificing her dreams at the altar of the upper crust.

"You four could double date." Her mother rubbed her manicured hands together, practically salivating onto her salad plate. "I'm sure if Brooke could find a nice young man instead of the degenerates she seems to gravitate to, she'd settle down and get married, maybe start a family."

"I've found a nice young man," Brooke blurted without thinking, wishing as soon as the words were out of her mouth that she could yank them back. Where in holy freaking hell had that come from? Not two seconds after vowing to compartmentalize her life and she'd already let Eli escape from his damn box.

Her mother's head snapped up like someone had mentioned a sale at Barneys. "Who is he? Do we know him? What does he do? Is it serious? Why didn't you bring him?"

Five questions without taking a breath. Another record. Her mother was in rare form today, even for her, and she wasn't going to be satisfied until Brooke threw her a bone or two.

Brooke reached for her half-empty glass. Where was that waiter? She needed that juice-less refill like yesterday. "Which one of those do you want me to answer first?"

Her mother waved a hand. "Take your pick."

Fine. She'd give her mother enough information to make her squirm. "His name's Eli Ward."

"The real estate developer?" her father said, sounding positively gleeful. "One of *Fortune's* forty under forty most influential people in business?"

"He and his sister run a charitable foundation," her mother added. "Something about girls and science. Such a worthy cause. We're hosting their black-tie fundraiser next month at the hotel. I expect you'll join us."

Brooke drained the last of her drink. "Not my Eli. Sorry to disappoint you, but Ward's a pretty common name."

Her Eli. She tried to ignore the frisson of excitement the words sent through her. *Not mine. We're not in a relationship.*

"How did you two meet?" Mallory asked.

Abort, abort. Brooke was so not going there with her parents in earshot. That sordid tale would only confirm her mother's worst fears about her disreputable daughter. "He's my neighbor. He moved in a few weeks ago."

She was saved from any more of her family's version of the Spanish Inquisition by the simultaneous appearance of their waiter and the dinging of her cell phone. She glanced at the screen and saw a text from Charise.

Mom sick. Can you watch Jaden? Boss says he'll fire me if I'm late one more time.

Hallelujah. A genuine emergency. A miracle on par with the loaves and the fishes. Or 1980's "Miracle on Ice" United States men's Olympic hockey team.

She banged out a quick text to let Charise know she was on her way and stood. "I'm sorry to cut this short, but I have to get back to Brooklyn. My neighbor's in trouble."

"Eli?" her mother asked, her lips pursing in disapproval.

"I do have other neighbors, you know." For now. Rumors had been swirling that a potential buyer was sniffing around Candy Court. But Brooke was ready for him, whoever he was. She'd already contacted the preservation commission about having the hundred-year-old building designated a historic landmark. If that effort was successful, the new owner would have his hands tied when it came to renovations. Without the threat of a major overhaul, hopefully Brooke and the other tenants would be allowed to stay and live in peace.

She threw down a twenty-dollar bill and hitched her hobo bag over her shoulder. "That should more than cover my share."

Her father pushed it back toward her, a game they played at all of their monthly brunches. She ignored it. "Until next time. It was nice meeting you, Hunter."

Not.

Her sister mimed a phone with her thumb and pinkie finger, held it up to her ear, and mouthed, "Call me."

Brooke mouthed back, "Will do," and headed to the coat check to retrieve her jacket before either of her parents could protest. She needed to talk to her baby sister about her less than stellar taste in men, that was for sure. And soon.

But first she had a baby to sit.

Chapter Eight

Fifteen minutes alone with the kid, and Eli was already sure of two things. One, babies ate a lot. And two, everything they ate, they either spit up or shat out.

He stripped off his puke-stained shirt and checked his watch again. It was up to eighteen minutes now. Eighteen long, excruciating minutes since Charise had banged on his door and begged him to come sit with Jaden until Brooke got back from Manhattan.

He didn't know she'd gone into the city. Not that she needed to apprise him of her every move. He was confident enough not to control the women he dated. If that's what he and Brooke were doing.

At some point, they'd have to figure it out. But that meant he'd have to come clean about who he was and why he was there, and he wasn't sure how he was going to do that without risking whatever it was they had together. Especially now that he'd signed a letter of intent for the Hearthstone Group—the new LLC he'd formed—to buy Candy Court. If that cheating bastard Simon had the balls to try to enforce the non-compete clause in their partnership agreement—well, Eli would let their lawyers hash that out.

He couldn't wait for the mess at Momentum to get cleared up. He'd hired a private investigator to tail Dupree, hoping that would lead to the mole, but so far he'd come up empty. If Eli didn't act fast on Candy Court, someone else would. The building was too good a deal to pass up.

But so was Brooke. She was the real deal. A woman who saw him for who he was, not what kind of car he drove or how much he had in his bank account or who he could introduce her to. Instead of going to stuffy museums and expensive restaurants, they'd spent the past few weeks discovering Brooklyn's simpler pleasures—and their nights discovering each other's bodies. So far, everything he'd uncovered he liked, about the borough and the bartender. More than liked, if he was being truthful.

Eli raked a hand through his hair and swore under his breath. How the hell had he gotten himself into this impossible situation? And how the hell was he going to get out of it with his business—and his manhood—intact?

A piercing wail brought him back to the problem at hand.

"All right, big guy." Eli tossed his shirt into the sink to be rinsed out later—good thing it was one of Ginny's Wal-Mart specials and not a designer label—and plucked a freshly wiped and diapered Jaden out of his bouncy seat. "Let's try this again."

Second time had to be the charm. After a little bit of fumbling with the bottle Charise had thrust in his hand on her way out the door, he settled onto one of the chairs at her tiny kitchen table, cradling Jaden against his bare chest. The kid wasn't going to get him this time if he could help it. "Okay, buddy. I ditched the shirt. Try to steer clear of the pants."

He nestled the baby's head in the crook of his arm and held the bottle to his lips. He'd never fed a baby before, but it didn't seem that hard, except for the whole spitting up thing. Something that, according to Google, was easily remedied by periodic burping.

Jaden's squalling stopped, and he latched onto the bottle, his little cheeks caving in with the effort of sucking down milk as fast as he could. Eli tilted the bottle upward—another trick he'd learned in his Google search—and stared down. Kids weren't something he'd spent a lot of time thinking about. He'd always assumed he'd find the right woman and get around to having one or two someday, but with his busy career, that day was in the distant future. Suddenly—shockingly—that future didn't seem so distant anymore. And the woman in it was a smart-mouthed, curvy brunette.

The doorknob clicked, and Eli looked up to see said brunette burst into the room, frazzled but still beautiful, her hair streaming behind her and her face red from the still chilly early-March air. "Ohmigod, Charise, I hope I'm not too late. The D-train took forever to show up and..."

Her eyes found him, and she stopped mid-sentence. Her oversize bag fell to the floor with a heavy thud, making him wonder what the hell she kept in there.

"Not Charise," he said with a wicked grin.

"I can see that." Her gaze lingered on the baby snuggled against his bare chest, and he thought he heard her mumble something about her ovaries exploding.

He choked back a laugh. "Sorry, I didn't catch that."

Her reddened cheeks flushed even more. "What can I say? A shirtless man feeding a baby. It's ridiculously hot."

"Any shirtless man?" He shifted Jaden to his other arm.

"I plead the fifth." She scanned the apartment. "Where's Charise?"

"She had to get to work. I offered to fill in until you got here."

"Offered?" Brooke unbuttoned her coat and hung it over

the back of a chair. "Or was drafted?"

"Now it's my turn to plead the fifth."

"I suppose she made you take your shirt off, too. Or was that your idea?"

"No, that was this little fellow." He glanced down at Jaden, who was still slurping away like a champ. "We had a slight accident our first go-round."

She took a seat opposite him. "Pee, poop, or puke?"

"All of the above."

"Ouch." She held out her arms. "Why don't you let me take over?"

The bottle was almost empty, and Jaden's eyes were drooping. Eli pried the nipple out of his mouth and moved him to his shoulder. "I'm fine."

"You sure are." Her gaze strayed back to his chest before returning to meet his. "But that's beside the point. The cavalry's here. You're relieved from duty."

"If you insist." He handed over the sleepy baby. "Want me to stick around? I could burp him or bathe him or something."

Or tell you who I am.

He slapped that thought down. It was too soon. He wasn't close to owning the building yet. A million things could happen to squash the deal. Until he was sure of the outcome, he was keeping his mouth shut. Why stir up unnecessary problems?

Brooke expertly transferred Jaden to her shoulder and began patting his back. "Don't you have some place better to be?"

"Nowhere I can think of." The truth of his words surprised him, and not in a bad way. They were back to playing house, but this time with a little addition to their faux family. Like a dutiful father, he picked up a dishtowel and held it out to her. "You might want to use this. Trust me. He's prolific. And he's got a range that rivals an ICBM."

"Thanks." She took the towel and draped it over her

shoulder. "He's about to pass out. We could watch a movie after I put him down. I know where Charise keeps her DVDs. With any luck, she's got something other than *Sesame Street* and *Baby Einstein*. Or I can run to my place and pick something from my stash."

"As long as it has a car chase, an explosion, or a completely gratuitous sex scene. Bonus points for all three."

"So no chick flicks?"

He shuddered. "Heaven forbid."

"Fine. I'll save *Crazy, Stupid, Love* for another day. Although it has like the best, most epic fight scene ever." The baby let out a loud burp. Brooke gave him one last pat and wiped his mouth with the towel.

"I'll make it up to you. I saw some microwave popcorn in the cabinet when I was looking for a bib."

"Butter flavor?"

"I think so."

"Then consider us even." She stood, crossed the open loft, and put the now fully asleep Jaden in his bassinet. "And for the love of God, put a shirt on."

"What's wrong?" He rose to join her, coming up behind her and banding his arms around her waist. "Too distracting for you in all my half-naked male glory?"

She leaned her head back against his shoulder, a teasing smile playing around the corners of her lips. "I have a hard time keeping my hands off you when you're fully dressed. Half naked it's practically impossible."

He inhaled the soft scent of her shampoo. Orange blossoms and coconut. "Who said you had to keep your hands off me?"

"In case you've forgotten, there's a baby in the room."

"He's sleeping." Eli turned Brooke in his arms so she faced him and rested his forehead against hers. "And I'm not suggesting we get busy on Charise's couch. But a good, old-fashioned make-out session's not going to scar the kid if he wakes up."

She sighed, the low, breathy sound going straight to his groin. "We'll see."

He bent to touch his lips to hers, but she stopped him with a not-so-subtle shove to the chest, forcing him to take a step back. For a split second, he thought he'd offended her, until he saw the mischievous sparkle in her bright, green eyes. "But not until you put on a damn shirt. Otherwise I can't guarantee we'll stop at kissing."

• • •

The fitted white T-shirt Eli returned in was only slightly less distracting than his magnificently naked chest, but Brooke supposed it would have to do.

The day had definitely taken a turn for the better. Not that it was possible for it to get much worse than the disastrous brunch with her parents. But walking in on Eli, shirtless and sexy, holding Jaden like he was the most precious thing in the world...*yowza.* It hadn't hurt that he'd looked completely at home doing it, feeding the kid like a pro. She could almost imagine him with their child...

Stop. Do not pass go. Do not collect two hundred dollars. What was wrong with her? In the span of a subway ride, she'd gone from swearing off relationships to having his baby, just from watching him wield a bottle. Without a shirt.

Swoon.

"How's this?" her fantasy baby daddy asked, strutting into the apartment and striking a hilariously bad runway model pose that he somehow managed to make look hot. Of course, she thought pretty much everything he did looked hot, so who was she to judge? "Think you can control yourself around me?"

"I'll do my best." She held up a DVD case. "*Lethal Weapon* okay?"

"Wait, we're seriously watching a movie? I thought we were going to have a little face time. And I'm not talking about on our iPhones."

She gave his shoulder a playful push. "You have a one-track mind."

He rocked back and forth on the balls of his feet, a self-satisfied smirk plastered across his face. "Is that a complaint or a compliment?"

She nudged him toward the sofa. "Sit down and shut up, and maybe you'll get lucky."

"What about the popcorn?"

"I figured we'd skip that. Nothing kills the mood more than kernels stuck in your teeth."

"Can't disagree with you there. I'd suggest a glass of wine, but we're on baby duty."

If her ovaries weren't toast already, they were now. Apparently maturity and a sense of responsibility were her new aphrodisiacs. "Charise usually keeps iced tea and bottled water in the fridge."

"Iced tea sounds great."

To her, too. Eli made himself comfortable on the couch while Brooke did a quick check on Jaden—still out cold—then got their drinks and popped the DVD into the player.

"Ready?" She grabbed the remote and settled down next to him.

"For anything." He put an arm around her and scooted her closer, dropping a kiss on the top of her head.

She pointed the remote at the TV and pressed play. The opening credits scrolled across the screen, and *Jingle Bell Rock* blasted through the tinny TV speakers. She frantically lowered the volume. "Don't want to wake the baby."

Eli trailed a finger down her arm from her elbow to

her wrist, a casual gesture that spoke volumes and sent an avalanche of tingles racing through her body. "We sure as hell don't."

Brooke sat back, resting her head against his shoulder, and tried to concentrate on the movie. No easy task, with his hand idly tracing a path up and down her arm and his breath stirring the hair at her temple and his heart beating a steady tattoo she could feel through her sweater. Not to mention his rock-hard thigh pressed against hers.

She reached for her glass of tea on the military-style foot locker Charise had cleverly converted into a coffee table, hoping it would cool her down and stop her from climbing onto Eli's lap and straddling him. Letting him help babysit wasn't her brightest idea, on par with the time she brought her mother's one-of-a-kind sapphire-and-diamond bracelet to school for show-and-tell. He was so close, and he looked and felt and smelled so good. Like cedar and sandalwood, a heady combination. What had made her think she could keep her hormones in check around him, even with his stupid shirt on?

She drained her glass and put it back on the makeshift table. With a groan, she stretched out her legs in front of her, flexing her toes in her boots.

"Long day?" he asked.

"You can say that again."

His hands moved to her shoulders, kneading the tight muscles of her back and neck. "That bad?"

"I'd rather not talk about it." She wasn't wading into that minefield. Talk about a mood-killer. Ten thousand times worse than a few harmless kernels of popcorn wedged between the incisors. She closed her eyes, let her head fall back, and groaned again. "Damn, that feels good."

"That's the general idea." He fingered the neckline of her cardigan. "It'll feel better if you lose this."

"Be my guest."

She held her arms out, and he peeled the sweater off. He laid it over the back of the couch and put one hand on either side of her spine, massaging in parallel lines all the way down her back to the top of her buttocks. Then he slid his hands back up to her neck, over her shoulders, and down her arms to her fingertips, his touch light and teasing.

She shivered, her girl parts jumping up and down and doing flips. "Where did you learn to do that?"

"I dated a girl who was a physical therapist for the Rangers."

"I'll bet she got you free tickets, too."

"On occasion."

"Nice fringe benefits."

His voice deepened, and he put his lips to her ear. "She's got nothing on you."

Without warning he bent, picked up her foot and pulled off her boot.

"What on earth are you doing?"

"What does it look like I'm doing?" He did the same with her other foot. "Taking your shoes off."

"That's obvious. Why?"

He lifted her stockinged feet and laid them over his lap. "No massage would be complete without a foot rub."

"Oh."

He grinned. His talented fingers had worked magic on her shoulders, neck, and back, but what they were doing now was pure heaven. Her toes curled involuntarily, and her feet arched into his hands.

"You don't have to do this."

"I know. I want to."

He worked his fist into the ball of her foot, and she drew in a quick breath. "God, that's the most amazing feeling ever."

"Really?" He slid his hand up her leg. "The most amazing? Better than my mouth on your breast? Or my cock in your…?"

"Stop." She held up a hand, cutting him off, and looked pointedly at Jaden's crib. "Don't tempt me with what I can't have."

"There's always tonight." His hand slid a little higher. "What time does Charise get off work?"

"Not soon enough."

"Well, sex maybe be out of the immediate picture, but there's nothing stopping us from doing this."

He took her legs from his lap and turned her to her side, stretching out with her and hovering over her like a panther waiting to pounce. Time seemed to stop with his hard edges molded to her soft curves, his mouth millimeters from hers, those ice-blue eyes studying her with an intensity that stole her breath and made rational thought impossible.

"What are you waiting for?" she asked, her ability to form a coherent sentence surprising her.

"I thought I heard something."

She turned her head toward the bassinet. "The baby?"

"I'm not sure."

They stayed that way for a minute, pressed together in a kind of torturous sexual limbo, listening to the hiss of the radiator and the steady hum of the midday traffic three floors below.

She turned back to him. "Whatever it was, it's gone now."

"Good."

This time the panther pounced without waiting, latching his mouth onto hers and teasing her lips with his tongue. She tunneled her fingers through his hair and let herself get lost in the kiss. She couldn't remember when she'd felt so deliciously wicked. It was like she was a teenager again, sneaking her boyfriend over for a few stolen kisses while she was babysitting.

He ground against her, and the evidence of his arousal

pressed into her hip. Yep. Her teenage years, all over again. Except now she knew exactly what she was missing. She knew how he'd feel inside her, how he'd start off nice and easy and then pick up the pace, pumping faster and harder until…

Bang. Bang. Bang.

She tensed and broke off the kiss. "Okay, that I heard."

"Open up." David's voice came through loud and clear from the other side of the door. "I know you're in there."

"David," Eli mouthed.

"He means we know you're in there," Chris corrected.

"And Chris," Brooke whispered.

"We can hear you talking," David said.

"And moaning," Chris added.

"I think there was more panting than moaning."

One of them laughed.

"What do you suppose they want?" Brooke asked, keeping her voice low.

"No clue." Eli gazed down at her and picked up where he'd left off, his body moving against hers. "But maybe if we ignore them long enough they'll go away."

Bang. Bang. Bang.

"We're not going away," Chris shouted. "No matter how long you ignore us."

"Somebody's got big ears," Eli complained.

"Come on, you guys," David said, sounding whiny even for him. "It's an emergency."

"All right, all right." Brooke sat up, taking a reluctant Eli with her. "But quit banging. You'll wake the baby."

As if on cue, Jaden whimpered.

Eli stood and adjusted his jeans. "I'll get the door. You get the kid."

"This better be good." Brooke tugged down the skirt of her dress and went to check on the baby.

"Oh, it is." Chris swept into the room with David close

behind him. "We're getting married."

"In two weeks," David added.

"That's great news." Brooke popped a binky in Jaden's mouth, which seemed to settle him down, then gave both men a bear hug. "I'm so happy for you."

"Congratulations." Eli slapped Chris on the back and shook David's hand. "But what's the rush?"

"Chris booked a tour with the American Ballet Theatre." David loped an affectionate arm around his fiancé's shoulders. "He'll be gone for six months."

Chris looked at David with a mix of tenderness and desire that made Brooke's heart ache. Had Eli ever looked at her that way? Had anyone? "We want to get married before I leave."

"That's where you guys come in." David eyes bounced from Brooke to Eli then back again. "We need your help."

Brooke cataloged the million things they'd need to accomplish to put on a wedding in that short amount of time. Invitations, flowers, food, music… "It's a stretch, but I think we can pull it off. The hardest part will be finding a venue."

"What about the rooftop garden?" Eli suggested.

"That's a great idea," agreed David.

Brooke frowned. "I don't know. It's coming along, but there's still a lot of work to do."

"We'll get the others to help, too," Chris said. "If we all pitch in, we'll have it looking fabulous in no time."

"It's only March," she pointed out. "It'll be cold up there."

"We can get portable heaters. I know a guy who'll hook us up cheap." Eli already had his cell out, his thumbs flying over the keyboard.

"I can see it." David rubbed his hands together. "A string quartet. Chinese lanterns. Orange and yellow snapdragons on every table. It'll be perfect."

Chris stilled David's hands, taking them in his own. "It'll

be perfect no matter what color flowers we have. Because I'm marrying my best friend."

They shared a tender, lingering kiss, and Brooke's heart cracked a little bit more. Chris was right. They were perfect together. So beautiful. They complemented each other, completed each other like two halves of a whole.

She slid a glance in Eli's direction. He leaned against the doorjamb, looking at David and Chris with the same reverence she imagined was in her eyes. Did he want what they had? Did she? What about her five-year plan?

"What do you say, Brooke?" Eli asked, his voice cutting into her thoughts. "Are you in?"

"Yeah, Brooke," David echoed. "Are you in?"

She swallowed the lump in her throat. "How can I say no to true love?"

Chapter Nine

"David asked me to bring this stuff up to you before he left." Charise held several strings of white lights in one arm and a matching bolt of tulle under the other. "Where do you want it?"

"Over there." Brooke pointed to Eli, who stood on a ladder under the canopy frame he'd built from PVC pipe, where, in a couple of days, David and Chris would say their vows. He'd proved surprisingly handy for a desk jockey. When she asked him about it, he'd brushed it off, repeating his claim about flipping houses back in the day. "How's the seating chart coming?"

Charise wrinkled her nose. "The list of who won't sit with who is longer than the phone book. It's like an episode of *The Young and the Restless*."

"Let me know if you need any help." Brooke shoveled a spade full of dirt around the base of a dwarf cypress and patted it down.

"I can handle it," Charise insisted. "You're busy enough as it is. But thanks for offering."

She delivered the lights and fabric to Eli and headed back downstairs.

Brooke put down her trowel and stood, surveying their progress. She was almost finished with the planter boxes. Eli had the canopy under control. Charise was dealing with the dreaded seating chart. David and Chris were off getting fitted for their tuxes. And the Feingolds were waiting in the lobby for the rental company to show up with the chairs and tables, probably squabbling the whole time over whose turn it was to take out the trash or whether the toilet paper was supposed to hang over or under the roll.

All in all, things were coming along nicely. Sure, there'd been the snafu with the photographer, who'd accidentally double-booked himself. And she had to call five florists before she found one who could track down snapdragons in the colors David specified. But they'd been minor inconveniences, swiftly handled.

The easiest call had been to the caterer. No one knew more about food—or weddings—than her sister. The Worthington had at least one a week, more during the busy months in the spring and fall. And Mallory had been more than happy to help David and Chris on their special day.

"Hey, Brooke," Eli called from his perch on the ladder. "Can you come over here and take a look at this?"

She wiped her dirt-covered palms on her jeans and went over to him. He'd fashioned a sort of curtain from the tulle, hanging it from the top of the canopy frame then gathering it and securing it to one corner with wide, silver ribbon.

The man was a marvel. Was there anything he couldn't do with those magic hands?

She banished all thoughts of his appendages—yes, that one, too—and gave him a thumbs-up. "Perfect."

"Great. I'll finish hanging the tulle and string the lights." Eli climbed down the ladder and moved it to the next corner, giving her butt a quick and dirty squeeze through her Levi's as he passed. She shot him a warning glare and looked around to make sure no one had joined them on the roof. A relieved sigh escaped her lungs when she saw they were still alone.

It wasn't like they were sneaking around. Hell, half of Candy Court had probably heard their bedroom antics on more than one occasion. The walls weren't three feet thick, and they weren't exactly quiet about it.

But sex in the privacy of one's own domicile was one thing. PDA was another. It somehow seemed more intimate. A declaration to the world that they belonged to each other. A declaration she wasn't sure either one of them was ready to make.

"Sounds like a plan." Brooke took a step back, needing to create some space between them, and gestured to the gardening tools and bag of potting soil she'd been using. "I'm going to put this stuff away and make sure the Feingolds haven't killed each other."

Before she could finish gathering her tools, the door to the roof swung open and Mallory stepped out into the surprisingly warm for mid-March sunshine.

"Mal." Brooke dropped the shears she was holding into a bucket. "What are you doing here?"

Mallory cocked her head then shook it. "Nice to see you, too."

"I'm surprised, that's all. You didn't text me you were coming. How did you get in the building?"

"The nice old couple downstairs let me in."

"Nice?" Brooke snorted. "They weren't at each other's throats?"

"Well, I'm pretty sure I interrupted something. But it wasn't an argument."

Brooke shuddered. "TMI, little sis. TMI."

"Forget I said anything."

"I'm not sure I can. The image is burned in my brain." Brooke grimaced. She needed to change the subject. Stat. "You never answered my original question. What brings you here?"

"I figured you could use an extra hand with the preparations. And I wanted to get a feel for the space before finalizing the menu."

"In that case..." Brooke picked up the bucket and handed it to her sister. "You can help me put this stuff back in the tool shed."

"Sure." Mallory shifted the bucket to her other arm. "Then maybe after we can...whoa."

Brooke followed her sister's gaze across the roof to Eli. He'd moved the ladder again and was a few rungs off the ground with his back to them. As he reached up to hang another panel, his shirt rode up, revealing a strip of golden skin above the waistband of his dangerously low-slung jeans.

Mallory let out a low whistle. "Please tell me that perfect ass belongs to your new neighbor."

"Did you just say ass?" Her sister never swore. Like, ever. And that included words like hell and damn.

"Now you're the one avoiding the question."

"What's wrong? Dr. McSnobby not enough for you?" They still hadn't had that talk about Hunter. Brooke reminded herself to make time for her sister once the wedding was in the rearview mirror.

"He's not that bad once you get to know him, honest." Mallory tapped the toe of one running shoe. "And you still haven't given me an answer."

"Fine, Little Miss Nosy Pants." Brooke hefted the bag of potting soil. "That's Eli."

"The guy you're banging?" Mallory tapped a finger against her cheek. "He doesn't look like a bean counter to me. More like a contractor. Or a Chippendales dancer."

"Jesus, Mal," Brooke hissed. She gave her sister the look of death and glanced over at Eli, who was thankfully still wrestling with the canopy. "Could you keep it down? And I never said I was banging him."

"But you are, aren't you?" Mallory asked with a smug smile. When did her sweet sister get so sassy? At least she'd managed to lower her voice a few decibels. "If you're not, you sure as heck should be."

Heck. Now that was more like the Mallory she knew. Except for the banging. Old Mallory would never refer to sex as banging. Old Mallory wouldn't refer to sex at all. At least not without blushing.

Brooke studied her sister's face. Her porcelain skin was flawless, as usual, not a hint of red or even a touch of pale pink in sight. "Who are you, and what did you do with my sister?"

"Consider this the new and improved Mallory Worthington." Her sister spread her arms and spun around, the bucket still dangling from one hand. "Call me Mallory two-point-oh."

"Okay, Mallory two-point-oh. Now that your curiosity has been satisfied, can we get rid of this stuff? This potting soil isn't getting any lighter."

"In a minute." She put the bucket down and threaded her way through the planter boxes across the roof.

"Hold up." Brooke dropped the potting soil and chased after her. "Where do you think you're going? The shed's the other way. And you forgot the bucket."

"I didn't forget it. I left it. I want to meet this man of yours."

"He's not mine," Brooke muttered.

"Right." There was that smug smile again. "You're just banging him."

"Enough with the banging."

"Fine. I'll be on my best behavior. Like you were with

Hunter."

Crap. That didn't bode well.

"Brooke." Eli caught her eye as they approached and climbed down from the ladder. "Who's your friend?"

"I'm her sister." Mallory stuck out her hand. "Mallory."

Eli gave Brooke a sideways glance, not trying to hide his shock. They hadn't talked much about families, his or hers. Her reasons were obvious. She didn't want to unload that mountain of baggage on him. She figured he had his reasons, too. And unlike her snoopy sister, it wasn't in her nature to pry.

"Eli." He shook Mallory's hand and gave her a smile that oozed confidence and charm. "Pleasure to meet you."

"Likewise." Mallory might not have blushed before, but she did now. Bowled over by the sheer force of Eli's magnetism, no doubt, like every other red-blooded female between the ages of eight and eighty. "I wish I could say I've heard all about you, but I'd be lying."

He chuckled and released her hand. "Same here."

"She's notoriously closemouthed," Mallory said, nodding in agreement. "When we were kids, she broke her wrist playing soccer and suffered in silence for three days before Carmen noticed her favoring it and brought her to the emergency room."

"She played soccer?"

Mallory waved her hand dismissively. "It was a brief dalliance. She spent more time chasing butterflies than the ball."

"Who's Carmen?" he asked.

"Our housekeeper."

Eli's eyes went wide, his surprise showing again. He must lose a fortune at poker. "Your family had a housekeeper?"

Danger, Will Robinson. Danger.

This little game of twenty questions had gone far enough.

Brooke had to stop it before her sister told Eli about the time she mooned the vice principal, or how she almost got busted for spray painting their neighbor's garage door. Or worse, outed her as one of the heirs to the Worthington hotel chain. People tended to treat her differently when they found out her family had a net worth somewhere in the mid seven figures. She hadn't told the other residents of Candy Court who she was until she'd lived there a year, and they were sworn to secrecy.

Brooke cleared her throat. "You two do realize I'm standing right here."

"Did you hear something?" Mallory put a hand to one ear.

Eli shrugged and stuck his hands in the pockets of his jeans. "Not me."

"Very funny." Brooke stepped between them and turned to her sister. "I thought you came here to help, not spill all our family secrets."

"Not all," Mallory teased, nudging Brooke with her elbow. "Just yours."

"And you." Brooke spun on Eli. "You're supposed to be working. This canopy isn't going to finish itself."

"I could use a hand." Eli gestured to the pile of tulle next to the ladder. "This is really a two-person job."

"I can help," Mallory offered.

Not. Gonna. Happen.

"I'll work with Eli," Brooke jumped in, nipping her sister's not-so-bright idea in the bud. The last thing she wanted was to give those two more time to swap stories. "You can go downstairs and keep an eye on the Feingolds. Then when Chris and David get back from their fitting, you can put the finishing touches on the menu with them."

"I see what you're doing." Mallory waved a finger at her. "And I'll go along with it. For now. But you can't keep us apart forever."

Brooke took her by the shoulders, turned her around, and nudged her toward the door. "Watch me."

"See you later, Eli," Mallory called over her shoulder. "Ask Brooke to tell you what happened to the class hamster in second grade."

The door clicked shut after her, echoing across the roof.

"So." Eli slid his arms around her. Hers settled on his chest, and he pulled her closer until she could feel every ridge and valley of his body. For a brief moment she thought he was going to kiss her, but then he spoke, his breath warming her cheek and skimming down her neck. "What's this I hear about a hamster?"

• • •

"Sure you want to go through with this?" Eli asked two days later as he straightened David's bow tie and clapped a hand on his shoulder. "There's still time to change your mind. We could get an Uber to the airport and use those tickets to Santorini."

"Don't you dare." Chris appeared in the doorway to Eli's apartment, where David was getting ready to march down the aisle. "It took me two years to convince him to marry me. I'm not letting him out of it that easy. And I'm sure as hell not letting you go on our honeymoon with him."

"What are you doing here?" David wailed, his tone of voice somewhere between a screech and a scream. He ducked behind Eli in a futile attempt to hide. "It's bad luck for us to see each other before the ceremony."

"We had breakfast together this morning," Chris pointed out.

"That doesn't count," David insisted to Eli's back. "It was ages ago."

"Eight hours is not ages."

"It is in my book."

"Boys, boys." Eli moved to one side, leaving David exposed. "No fighting on your wedding day. You're both pretty."

Chris put his hands in the pockets of his tuxedo pants. "We're not fighting, we're arguing."

"Which we wouldn't be doing if someone respected tradition and kept his distance." David narrowed his eyes at his soon-to-be husband.

"I thought I told you to stay downstairs." Brooke came up behind Chris and smacked him on the back of the head. "The two grooms aren't supposed to see each other before the wedding. It's bad luck."

"That's what I said." David huffed. "Not that anyone listens to me."

Eli certainly wasn't listening to him. How could he with Brooke standing there looking like a goddess in a short, figure-hugging black dress and gladiator sandals? A triple strand of pearls hung in the valley between her breasts. A matching bracelet adorned one bare arm, and she wore pearl and what he assumed were diamond studs in her ears. She'd left her hair hanging loose around her shoulders the way he liked it, making him itch to grab a handful and tilt her head to the perfect angle for him to kiss her into next week, wedding be damned.

"You look…" He searched for the right word and came up short, settling for the first thing that popped into his head. "Gorgeous."

"It's a gift." Chris tugged on the cuffs of his jacket and adjusted his cummerbund. "Or a curse."

"He's not talking to you, doofus." David rolled his eyes. "He's talking to her."

"Thanks." Brooke openly ogled Eli. "So do you."

He'd pulled out all the stops and had Ginny raid the closet at his penthouse. The result—a navy-blue suit he'd paired with a pale-pink dress shirt, burgundy tie, and matching pocket square for a pop of color. Every guy had at least one good outfit in his wardrobe for special occasions, right?

"Come on." Chris looped Brooke's arm over his. "Let's get out of here before my fiancé blows a gasket. Or one of you two heterosexual lovebirds spontaneously combusts from all this pent-up sexual tension."

"I need you guys on the roof in ten minutes," Brooke called over her shoulder as he dragged her off. "The guests are almost all here."

"Don't worry." Eli slipped David's tux jacket off the hanger. "We'll be there."

The door closed behind them. Eli held out David's jacket. "You ready?"

"As I'll ever be." David put his arms through the sleeves and fastened the top button. "You?"

"You're the one tying the knot, my friend, not me." Eli took David's boutonniere out of box and stuck the pin between his teeth.

David fixed his collar. "From the way you and Brooke practically eye-fucked each other, I wouldn't be surprised if you're next."

Eli laid the boutonniere flat against David's lapel. "Shut up and hold still."

"Charise says you two go at it like rabbits every night. Really noisy, nympho rabbits."

Shit. He knew they should have kept the moaning, groaning and oh-my-God-ing to a minimum. Not that either of them seemed to have any self-control when their clothes were off. Or on. "You really want to go there? I'm holding a long, sharp pin inches from your heart. And I'm not afraid to use it."

David's teasing smile faded into a thin line, and any trace of humor disappeared from his eyes. "In all seriousness, man, Brooke's special."

"I know." He wouldn't get any argument on that from Eli.

"We've been friends for almost three years. Ever since Chris and I moved into this building. More than friends, actually. She's like a sister to me." David hesitated, his next words coming out slow and measured. "I don't want to see her get hurt."

"Neither do I."

"Then don't you think it's time to tell her the truth?"

The pin in Eli's hand slipped, jabbing his index finger and falling to the floor. He jerked back and sucked his injured finger into his mouth. This was it. His day of reckoning. The shit had hit the fan.

He took a deep breath and tried to quell the flood of panic rising inside him, making his chest tighten. "What do you mean?"

"You're in love with her," David stated matter-of-factly, like he was discussing the weather. "Or well on your way to it."

Part of Eli sagged in relief. David didn't know his real identity, or his reason for being at Candy Court. It was important he tell everyone—especially Brooke—on his own terms, when the time was right. And that time was almost here.

But as relieved as he was that his secret was still safe, another part of him continued to panic. It was too soon to be throwing around the "L" word, wasn't it?

He repositioned the boutonniere. "What makes you say that?"

"It's as obvious as a bad boob job." David handed him a fresh pin. "All you have to do is look in a mirror. You've got all the classic symptoms. Yearning look. Dopey grin. Shortness of breath. The next thing you know you'll be doodling hearts and flowers on your spreadsheets. Or whatever it is you work with."

So much for his big-time-real-estate-magnate poker face. If David could read him like a cheap airport paperback, could everyone else? Could Brooke?

"We've barely known each other two months." The protest sounded lame, even to Eli's ears. He pushed the pin through the stem of the boutonniere and stepped back to observe his handiwork.

"Weeks, months, years. Love doesn't have a timetable. I moved in with Chris three weeks after we met." David shifted to the mirror to check his appearance. "Haven't you ever been in love before?"

Eli fiddled with his pocket square. "I thought so, back in college. But now I'm not so sure."

David gave his reflection a final once-over and turned back to Eli. "Yeah. The real thing will do that to you."

The real thing. The words tugged at Eli's conscience. It felt real. It felt right. But how right or real could it be until he was completely honest with her?

The door cracked open and Brooke stuck her head in. "Your ten minutes are up, and the natives are getting restless. Are we doing this, or what?"

"You bet your ass we're doing this," David said, his tone joking but his expression deadly serious. "I can't have Chris jeté-ing his way across Europe in tights and a dance belt without a ring on his finger. Which reminds me."

He took a small, square box out of his pants pocket and put it in Eli's palm. "Here. The rings. Don't forget them. And don't forget what we talked about."

Eli nodded. "I won't."

David breezed past Brooke, planting a kiss on her cheek as he went. "See you on the roof."

"What was that all about?" Brooke asked in his wake.

"Guy stuff." There wasn't time for even the abridged version of what he needed to say to her. That would have to come later. Eli crossed to Brooke and offered her his arm. "Shall we?"

She threaded her arm through his and let him lead her into the hallway and toward the stairs to the roof. "I'm all yours."

Chapter Ten

Brooke didn't cry at weddings. She didn't. The moisture gathering at the corners of her eyes as she watched David and Chris exchange vows wasn't tears. It was her damn ragweed allergy acting up again. In March.

"Here," Eli whispered, dangling a handkerchief from his fingertips.

"A handkerchief? Who still carries a handkerchief?" She took it, running her thumb over the "EWJ" embroidered in the corner. "And monogrammed, no less."

"They're extremely handy. Perfect for lending to damsels in distress."

"Do you come across a lot of those?"

He took her free hand and weaved his fingers with hers. "Only one, recently."

She dabbed at her eyes—stupid allergy—and turned her attention back to the ceremony. As happy as she was for David and Chris, who had finished with the vows and were exchanging rings, she couldn't help feeling a little wistful.

Things were finally starting to go her way. Her agent

had loved the last set of revisions. She lived in a great neighborhood, surrounded by good friends. And she had a hotter-than-hell guy in her bed every night who made sure she never went to sleep unsatisfied.

But how long would it last? Her book might never sell. Any day now, she and her friends could be out on the street. And as much fun as she was having with Eli, watching David and Chris stand before their family and friends and swear to have and to hold from this day forward, seeing the love and promise in their eyes as they slipped the rings onto each other's fingers, made her wonder if maybe she and Eli could have that, too.

"You okay?" he asked under his breath.

She nodded and stared straight ahead, not daring to look at him. Her face had always been an open book, and she was afraid of what he might see there now. "Allergies."

"Right." He drew out the word like he was savoring it.

"Screw you."

He chuckled and turned her hand over in his, running his thumb over her palm. The slight touch reverberated all the way to the tips of her toes in her high-heeled Roman sandals. "Later."

"Shh," Mr. Feingold hissed loudly, rapping Brooke on the shoulder. "I can't hear."

"Neither can anyone else now, thanks to you, old man," his wife scolded, her voice only slightly softer than her husband.

For the rest of the ceremony, Brooke kept her mouth shut and her eyes on the happy couple. No easy task with Eli refusing to release her hand, his thumb continuing to draw slow circles on her palm. How could such a simple, seemingly innocuous touch create such a tidal wave of sexual pleasure? It was a good thing they were sitting down because she didn't think her legs would support her.

Only when the service was over and David and Chris

shared their first—almost obscenely long—kiss as spouses for life did she sneak a glance at Eli. He looked right back and mouthed, "Later."

"One-track mind," she mouthed back. But at that moment, as David and Chris continued to kiss and Eli stared at her with a bittersweet smile, something deep inside told her they were talking about more than sex.

Cocktails and dinner passed in a sort of blur. By the time they'd eaten Mallory's fabulously prepared food and Charise's boyfriend du jour had started spinning tunes on Eli's sound system, Brooke had a nice little champagne buzz. She shook her booty to Beyoncé and Britney Spears and taught the Feingolds the Electric Slide before a slow song came on, one that called for lots of touching and swaying and romance. PDA of the highest degree.

"It's about time." Eli intercepted her at the edge of the makeshift dance floor and held out his hand. His jacket was long gone, and he'd rolled up his shirtsleeves to his elbows. "Dance with me."

It was a command, not a question. Brooke looked at his outstretched hand then met his gaze. It was what she saw there that made her overcome her deep-seeded aversion to public displays of affection. Not need or desire, but a kind of quiet desperation, as if his world would end if they didn't share this dance.

She took his hand and let him lead her past the other swaying couples to the center of the floor. His grip tightened, and he tugged her closer so he could slide his other arm around her waist. The heat of his palm on her back scorched her skin through the crepe of her dress. She let out a breath she hadn't realized she'd been holding and flattened her free hand against his chest.

"It was a beautiful wedding," she said lamely, her eyes fixed on one of his shirt buttons.

"Thanks to you." The hand at her back pressed more firmly against her until their hips brushed with every step.

"And you."

He dipped his head so his lips skimmed her earlobe. "What do you say we get out of here?"

She pulled back far enough to look at him. "Wouldn't that be rude?"

She followed his gaze to David and Chris, locked in each other's arms on the opposite side of the dance floor, oblivious to everything but themselves. "Somehow I don't think they'll miss us."

"What about my sister?" She scanned the rooftop for Mallory and spotted her helping one of the waiters cut and plate the cake.

"What about her?" He pulled her back to him and pressed his cheek to hers. Under her palm, his heart beat as wildly as hers.

She closed her eyes and listened to the music. Eric Clapton's "Wonderful Tonight." Fitting. The night had been pretty darned wonderful. She sighed and let go of her last shred of doubt, letting herself drown in the music and the moment and the man. "I told her I'd help with the cleanup."

"She's got staff. You've done enough." Eli spun her around in a slow circle so she could take it all in. The sun, which had been setting during the ceremony, was long gone, and the white LEDs twinkled against the backdrop of the cloudless blue-black sky. "Look at this place. You transformed a half-finished garden into a rooftop paradise."

"Like I said, I had help."

"Every team needs a leader."

His cheek brushed her hair, and his hand slid up her back in a gentle caress. He shifted his grip on her hand so his thumb was back to its old tricks, teasing her palm with soft circles. Like before, the simple touch set off a tsunami inside her.

"Okay, let's go." She rested her cheek against his shoulder. "But I have to let my sister know I'm leaving. And I'm grabbing us a couple of pieces of cake. It's chocolate almond, with raspberry mousse and a chocolate ganache. I never pass up chocolate."

"I like the way you think." He dropped a kiss on the top of her head that should have been platonic but only served to whip her already crazed hormones into a frenzy. "I'll snag a bottle of champagne and meet you at my place in five minutes."

"Why your place?"

"It's about twenty feet closer. And I don't want to wait any longer than necessary to have you naked and underneath me."

"You sure know how to sweet-talk a girl." She toyed with a button on his shirt, two fingers slipping between what felt like two-hundred-thread-count Egyptian cotton to stroke his bare flesh. Two could play this game. "But who says I'll be underneath you?"

His eyes darkened to a velvety blue, and the heartbeat under her hand stuttered. "Good point."

He slid a finger under her chin, lifted her face to his, and kissed her again. No prelude, no hesitation, nothing platonic about it this time. He dipped his head to hers and claimed her mouth like it was his for the taking, no matter where they were or who was watching.

When he was finished, he stepped back, brushed a loose hair behind her ear, and headed for the bar, leaving her dazed and wanting in the middle of the dance floor. Heart pounding, she navigated on shaky legs through the crowd of dancers and found Mallory still doling out cake.

"That was some kiss," her sister said, not wasting any time getting into the thick of things.

"Oh. You saw."

"Everyone saw. You two weren't exactly subtle." Mallory continued to cut and plate cake, her knife working quickly and efficiently. "This guy must be special. I thought you hated PDA."

"If I take off, will you be okay cleaning up without me?" Brooke asked, ignoring her sister's implication.

"Fine. Don't answer me. And yes, you can go get down and dirty with your new boy toy. I've got plenty of help." Mallory handed her two pieces of cake. "Get out of here."

"You know I love you." Brooke took both plates and grabbed a third for good measure. "Lunch Tuesday? Anywhere but Heirloom."

"Sounds good. I'll text you."

Carefully balancing the cake plates, Brooke made her way down the stairs to Eli's apartment. The door was open a crack, so she shouldered her way through, set the plates down on the counter that separated the kitchen from the rest of the apartment, and untied her sandals so she could pull them off. Why she'd thought she could wear those things for more than an hour without killing her feet was a mystery. She leaned against the counter and wiggled her relieved toes. Maybe she could convince Eli to give her another foot rub. Without any interruptions.

"What took you so long?"

His voice drifted across the apartment, lit by a solitary lamp. She turned to see him sitting in shadow on the bed. He'd already stripped off his tie, which lay discarded on the floor, and was working on the buttons of his shirt.

She took a step toward him. "Not wasting any time, I see."

"I told you." The shirt hit the floor next to the tie, and he started on his pants, sliding his belt from its buckle. "I'm not waiting one second longer than necessary to fuck you."

"Then I'd better get naked." Her fingers found the zipper at the back of her dress and pulled it down. She could feel his eyes on her as she slipped it off her shoulders, wriggled it down to her feet and kicked it to one side, leaving her standing in front of him in only a lacy black demi bra and a thong.

He stood and shucked off his pants, his hungry eyes continuing to roam over her. "Come here."

She returned the favor, her gaze eating him up like he was a decadent, seductive desert, yummier than the chocolate almond cake that sat all but forgotten on the counter. Christ, he was magnificent, all lean muscle and smooth skin. "Make me."

"So that's how you want to play it." He lay on the bed, leaning back on his elbows. "I didn't know you liked it rough."

She didn't, but now that he'd mentioned it, the idea of shifting the balance of power in the bedroom, letting him take the reins, had a certain appeal.

She spotted his tie out of the corner of one eye and bent to pick it up.

Looping the silk around her neck, she moved between his splayed legs, putting her hands on his shoulders and bending over to whisper in his ear. "I want you to blindfold me."

• • •

Beautiful. Sexy. Confident.

Those words barely scratched the surface of the exquisite creature standing before him, loud and proud and so damn perfect he ached to touch every inch of her. But it wasn't the pouty breasts that hung inches from his mouth or the neatly trimmed landing strip of dark hair pointing the way to the promised land that wrecked him.

It was her vulnerability. Knowing she trusted him enough to relinquish control had him teetering on the edge.

He felt a momentary pang of guilt. He didn't deserve her trust. But that was going to change. He had a new plan for

Candy Court, one that had started forming as he'd watched the residents come together to make Chris and David's wedding day one they'd never forget. A plan he hoped would help Brooke overlook the fact that he hadn't been entirely truthful about his identity or his intentions. Once the ink was dry on the contracts and there was no way Dupree—or anyone else—could sneak in under the wire, he'd lay all his cards on the table and tell her everything.

But he didn't have to wait until then to prove himself to her. He could start earning her trust now by giving her what she'd been brave enough to ask for.

"Are you sure?" He fingered one end of the tie around her neck.

She took it off, placed it in his open palm, and closed his fingers around it. "I'm sure."

He gestured to the bed. "Lie down."

She obeyed, lying on her back.

He joined her, straddling her hips. "Ready?"

She nodded. He lifted her head and secured the blindfold. "Too tight?"

She drew her lower lip into her mouth. "No."

"Trust me. It'll be good." He dipped his head to her neck and dragged his lips along her collarbone. His hardening dick brushed her soft folds, already wet with her arousal. Torture. Sweet, fucking torture. "Eliminating one sense heightens the others."

"You don't say." She shivered as his mouth opened to softly suck the skin at the top of one breast between his teeth. "Tell me more."

"I'd rather show you."

His hands cupped her face, and his mouth closed over hers in a kiss that was both passionate and possessive. He coaxed her lips open, and his tongue swept in to tangle with hers. He kissed her for long, leisurely minutes until they were both panting and desperate, then gentled the kiss and pulled back.

"You taste fucking amazing." He pressed a kiss to her jawline. "Here."

Her chest rose and fell rapidly, and her hands fisted in the rumpled comforter. His mouth moved to her breast. He swiped the nipple with his tongue. "And here. Sweet. Clean."

She gave a soft moan and arched beneath him. "I didn't know."

"Know what?"

"That not being able to see you would be so…"

"Yes?" His hand joined his mouth at her breast, his fingers working in conjunction with his lips, toying with her nipple.

"Frustrating." Her hands tightened their hold on the bedspread. "Intense."

He lifted his head to look at her. "Good intense, or bad intense?"

"Good." She sighed. "Definitely good."

"It's about to get better."

He slid down her body until his head was level with her belly and his hands were on her inner thighs. His tongue circled her belly button as he pressed her legs apart. "Does it turn you on, not being able to see what I'm doing? Not knowing where I'll touch you next? Whether I'll use my hands or my mouth?"

She moistened her lips and nodded.

That was all the invitation he needed. He didn't waste any time tasting her intimately, using the entire length of his tongue to devour her in long, slow strokes.

"So wet," he murmured against her, adding a finger, then two, moving them in and out as he sucked on her sweet spot. "So tight."

She writhed beneath him.

He raised his head and let his eyes roam up her body,

soaking in every lush, lovely inch of her. "I need to be inside you."

"Yes," she panted, pressing her hips up to meet his probing fingers. "I want that, too."

He rolled off her and reached for a condom on the bedside table. In seconds, he'd rolled it on and was back on top of her, his aching dick poised at her entrance.

"Now." She hooked one leg around his waist. "Please, now."

He stared down at her, watching her face as he slid inside her. His hips began to move, and Brooke wrapped both legs around him, urging him forward.

Eli pushed into her, setting a slow, steady rhythm. She met each thrust with a move of her own, bucking and writhing underneath him. Her nipples brushed against his chest, and his jaw clenched as he gradually picked up the pace. Their bodies moved in perfect rhythm as he plunged into her over and over, withdrawing every so often to tease her with the head of his cock before thrusting into her again.

He stilled with his cock buried deep inside her. "Tell me what you need."

"You know what I need." The edge in her voice made his balls tighten.

"Maybe." He swept a hand up her body to cup one breast, brushing his fingers over the nipple and watching it harden. "But I'd still like to hear it. You know, to be sure I'm getting it right."

"Oh, you're getting it right." She let her head fall back against the pillow, extending the long line of her neck. "Trust me."

He moved to the other breast, giving it the same treatment with the same result. "Tell me."

"Jerk."

"Yeah." He removed his hand and stared down at her as

she undulated against him, willing him with her body to finish her off. "But I'm the jerk that's going to give you what you need."

She let out a stifled moan.

"Why so shy all of a sudden?" he teased, reaching up and flicking one end of the tie covering her eyes. "You didn't have any trouble asking me to blindfold you."

"Fine, you win." Her head thrashed from side to side. "I need to come. Like, now."

"Ask, and you shall receive."

He moved inside her again, leaning back enough so he could watch his cock disappear and reappear. There was nothing more erotic than seeing them connected in the most intimate way possible. When he felt her start to spasm around him, he reached down and whipped off the necktie.

She turned her head and buried her face in the pillow.

"Don't hide from me." He brought a hand to her face and turned it back to him. "I want to see the look in your eyes when you come. They get all wide and dreamy, and your mouth forms this perfect little "o," like you're surprised every time it happens. It's a huge fucking turn-on."

Slowly, she opened her eyes, blinking up at him as she trembled and shook with the force of her orgasm. He followed right after, spilling his own release inside her. When he was done, he rolled to his side, taking her with him. She laid her head on his shoulder, the rapid rise and fall of her chest gradually slowing as she recovered.

"So, now I know." One leg tangled with his.

His breath caught at the openly possessive move. "Know what?"

"What all the fuss is about." She sighed and snuggled into him. "You were right. It does heighten all the other senses."

He smiled against her cheek as he stroked her hair and back. Her stomach rumbled, and he laughed. "Hungry?"

"Well, we did work up an appetite." She eyed the plates on the kitchen counter. "And there's three perfectly good slices of chocolate almond cake practically within arm's reach."

"I suppose you want dessert in bed."

"I wouldn't object." She raised her arms above her head, stretching like a cat and bringing all her fun parts into contact with his—breasts to chest, wet heat to hardening cock. His recuperative powers were strong with this one.

He bent to nip her lower lip. "How do you feel about food play?"

"Okay, I'll bite." She smoothed a hand down his belly, letting it rest on the curve of his hip, tantalizingly close to the V that led to his groin. "Pun intended. But only on one condition."

"What's that?"

In one swift, sudden move she flipped him onto his back and climbed on top of him, giving him a perfect view up her sleek torso to her ripe, round breasts. "This time you wear the blindfold."

Chapter Eleven

"To what do I owe this pleasure?" Ginny dropped her pocketbook on the floor, slipped off her coat, and slid into a chair opposite Eli at Dean & Deluca, a steaming cup in her hand that he knew would contain her beverage of choice—a half-sweet, non-fat caramel macchiato. "You haven't set foot on the island for weeks. I was starting to think I'd never see you again."

He hadn't been counting the days, but now that he thought about it, Ginny was right. Thanks to email, texting, and Skype, he'd been able to keep tabs on things without having to return to Manhattan since moving into Candy Court. And more surprising, he hadn't missed it one damn bit.

He smiled and sipped his way-less-complicated dark roast, black, with his usual two shots of espresso. "Would you believe me if I said I missed you?"

"No." She blew across the top of her cup, making waves in the thick foam.

He put a hand over his heart. "You wound me."

"You'll get over it." She licked some of the foam from

the rim of her cup and drank. "Your absence hasn't gone unnoticed. People have been talking."

"I didn't expect it would." He set his half-empty cup down on the table with a hollow *thunk*. "What people?"

"Simon. I don't think he's buying my story about the Tibetan monastery."

He leaned back in his chair, stretching his legs out and crossing them at the ankles. "You seriously went with that?"

"It seemed like a good idea at the time. Hard to prove one way or the other." She patted her silvery gray hair and loosened a button on her cardigan. "Then again, I didn't think you'd fall off the face of the earth for two months."

"Last time I checked, Brooklyn's still on terra firma. And it's not like we haven't been in constant contact."

"What's so important you broke your self-imposed exile and dragged me out of the office in the middle of the workday?" Ginny asked, clearly anxious to get to the purpose of their tête-á-tête. "Do you have a lead on our mole?"

"I was going to ask you that same question."

She shook her head. "Nothing yet. Mr. Spock should be sending me a status report any day now."

Eli raised a brow. "Mr. Spock? What is this, Star Trek?"

"Do you read my emails?" She clucked her tongue at him. "Gordon Spock. He's the private investigator who's been following Dupree."

"Yes, I read your emails," Eli insisted. "I've been a little busy lately."

"Busy? Or preoccupied?"

"Busy." He repeated the half-truth. Ginny didn't need to know how much time he'd been spending with Brooke. Or what they'd been doing. "With the Candy Court project."

"I've seen the architect's renderings." She blew into her coffee again and took another tentative sip. "Very ambitious."

"That's what I wanted to talk to you about." He bent

down and picked up a long cardboard tube from under the table. "There's been a change of plan."

He popped the cap off one end of the tube and slid out a rolled-up sheet of paper. He moved his coffee to one side and spread it out on the table.

Ginny fished her reading glasses out of her purse, perched them on her nose and squinted down at the drawing. "What's this?"

"Like I said, a change of plan."

The furrows in her forehead deepened as she studied the sketch in more detail, her finger tracing the clean lines. "Are you sure about this?"

"As sure as I've ever been about anything." The words left his mouth freely, easily. He was sure. Damn sure. He'd spent the week and change since the wedding working with the architect on the new drawings. He'd thought Eli was nuts, too, scrapping everything and starting from scratch on a design that wouldn't be anywhere near as profitable as the one they'd first agreed on. But for the first time in his business career, this deal wasn't about profit. It was about people.

Or, more accurately, one particular person.

"What gives?" Ginny stared at him like he had three heads and a tail. Maybe a set of wings, too. "Where's the real Eli Ward and what have you done with him?"

"He's sitting right in front of you, wondering if you've gone completely insane or you're suffering from caffeine overdose."

"I'm serious, Eli." She peered at him over her glasses, her voice gentle but firm. "This is nothing like what you originally had drawn up. If you do this, you'll be leaving a lot of money on the table."

He shrugged and stared down at his loafers. He hadn't worn them in weeks, yet for some reason, he'd felt compelled to put them on today. Same with his freshly pressed button-down and flat-front khakis. Hell, he'd worn a goddamn tie. Like putting on armor to do battle.

He retrieved his coffee and took a sip, savoring the taste and feel of the hot, dark liquid as it ran over his tongue and down his throat. "Money isn't everything."

"Now I know something is wrong. You're not sick are you?" She reached across the table and put a hand to his forehead. "Oh my God, that's it, isn't it? You're dying. You've got six months to live, and this is some sort of last ditch effort to make peace with your maker."

"It's nothing that melodramatic, I swear." He finished his coffee, crushed the cup in his hand, and tossed it into a nearby trash can. "Besides, aren't you the one always telling me the best things in life are free?"

"Yes. But I hadn't realized you were actually paying attention." Ginny's glasses slipped lower on her nose, and she pushed them up with her index finger. "Dare I ask what—or who—is responsible for this remarkable transformation?"

The answer to her question was obvious, but it wasn't one Eli was ready to give, even to the woman who'd become almost a mother to him. What he shared with Brooke was too new, too fragile, too uncertain.

"The building doesn't need to be razed, it needs to be restored." He tapped the drawing. "High ceilings. Exposed brick. Natural wood beams. If we do this right, it'll appeal to everyone from baby boomers to millennials. We'll be at full occupancy before the paint is dry."

"Fine." Ginny took off her glasses, snapped them shut and stowed them in her purse. "Don't tell me who she is. I'll figure it out eventually. I haven't worked for you for eight years without learning a few tricks."

He rolled up the plans and slid them back into the tube, glad to be done with the sensitive subject of his love life. At least for now. "Any word from the title insurance company?"

She pulled a manila folder from her pocketbook. "I've got the preliminary title report right here, along with the FEMA flood map and a summary of the applicable zoning regulations and permit requirements from the city planning department."

She slid the folder across the table to him. He opened it and leafed through the documents. "Good work, Ginny. Anything else?"

"Not that I can think of." She stood and started to put on her coat. "Oh, I sent your tuxedo out to be cleaned so it will be ready for the silent auction next week."

The auction. Shit. He'd all but forgotten about it. "Thanks. You'll be there, I hope."

"Wouldn't miss it. I know how important Geek Girls is to you and Paige." She hitched her purse over her arm. "Will you be bringing a date?"

He rose to join her, grabbing his coat from the back of his chair. "Nice try, but you're not going to worm it out of me that easily."

"Ah-ha." She jabbed a finger at him. "So, there is something to worm out of you."

Damn, the old bird was good. He slung an arm around her considerably smaller shoulders and steered her toward the door. "If there is, I'm not going to let it slip at a black-tie benefit with the grand dames of New York society looking on. Those women scare me. They're the real gossip girls."

Part of him—a big part—wanted nothing more than to stroll into the fundraiser with Brooke on his arm. But there was no way he could invite Brooke without blowing his cover, and he wasn't ready to do that yet.

He would be. Soon. Very soon. He just hoped when that time rolled around she'd be willing to listen to him.

• • •

"We've got trouble." David burst through Brooke's door, tanned and refreshed from his honeymoon and waving one arm excitedly.

"Knock much?" Brooke put down her pencil and rested her elbows on her drawing table. Since the wedding, she'd been more productive than ever. Her muse, which had deserted her, had returned with a vengeance. Like most creative types, she didn't want to overthink the reason for her sudden change of fortune. But it didn't take a rocket scientist to figure out what was different.

Her relationship with Eli. Okay, yeah, she'd used the word relationship. Shoot her. And she hadn't been hit by a stray comet or struck by lightning. Miracle of miracles.

It was like she and Eli had crossed a bridge that night after the wedding, from friends with benefits to a bona fide couple. They'd established a sort of new normal. Going about their own business during the day, which for her meant writing or drawing or pulling an occasional shift at Flotsam and Jetsam, and for him meant tabulating columns and organizing spreadsheets or whatever it was financial wizards did. Then it was takeout or dinner at a local restaurant, neither one of them being particularly adept in the kitchen. Well, adept at cooking. They'd found plenty of other, more creative, uses for the space, and about every other surface in their respective apartments

In between their marathon sex sessions, they'd watch movies, listen to music—aside from their shared affection for second British invasion bands, he preferred jazz fusion, she headbanging heavy metal—or talk about everything from politics to prime-time television, staying deftly away from their personal lives, which they avoided as if by tacit, unspoken agreement, his apparently being as messy as hers. When they were spent, from conversation or coitus, they'd fall asleep tangled in each other and wake the next morning to have breakfast together before starting the whole cycle over again.

The kind of normal a girl could get used to, if she let herself.

"No time for formalities." David smacked a hand down on her drafting table, scattering papers and snapping Brooke out of her Eli-induced daydream. "There's a guy outside with a tripod and some fancy electronic equipment, planting little flags everywhere."

Icy fingers of dread clawed at her gut. She swallowed hard and tried to tamp it down as she gathered the fallen papers and tossed them haphazardly on the table. She'd have to sort that mess out later. Right now, she had more a pressing predicament to deal with.

"It's probably someone from the gas company marking where the underground lines are." She crossed her fingers behind her back, hoping her tone was more optimistic than she felt.

David frowned. "His truck says Atlas Surveying and Mapping."

So much for optimism.

"Come on." She threw on an oversize sweatshirt over her usual writing attire—yoga pants and a graphic tee—and slipped into a pair of Ugg boots she'd left by the door. "Let's find out what's going on."

Half an hour and whole host of unanswered questions later, they were back in her apartment.

"Okay." Brooke paced the length of her studio, drumming her fingers together. "Let's summarize what we know."

"Not much." David pulled open the refrigerator door and peered inside. "Do you have anything to eat besides and white bread, mustard, and Italian dressing?"

"How can you think of food at a time like this?" She came up behind him and pushed the door closed.

"Chris did all the cooking. Ever since he left, I've been subsisting on ramen noodles and mac and cheese. A giant step down from my usual fare."

"He's only been gone two days."

"The two longest days of my life."

He leaned against the counter and let out a heavy sigh, looking so forlorn Brooke took pity on him and tossed him a granola bar from a box in the cabinet above the sink. "Here. This should tide you over until your next ramen fix."

"Thanks." He ripped off the wrapper and bit into it with a satisfied moan.

She closed the cabinet and leaned against the counter next to him. "Now can we get back to the matter at hand?"

"And what would that be?" Eli strode through the door, the smell of Thai spices wafting from the bag in his arms.

"Hallelujah. Real food." David came around the counter and took the bag from him.

Eli shrugged off his dark gray topcoat—the same one he'd been wearing the night they met, she remembered—and tossed it over the back of the couch. "Good thing I got enough for an army."

Brooke crossed her arms under her chest. "Again, with the no knocking. What is it with the people in this building?"

"What's the big deal?" David put the bag on the counter and started emptying it, laying out the contents in a neat, straight line. "He practically lives here anyway, and vice versa. You two might as well exchange keys."

Brooke scuffed the toe of her boot against the hardwood floor. He had a point about the keys. And maybe about the food, too. Things always looked better on a full stomach. She opened another cabinet, took out three plates, and placed them on the counter with the food.

"He's got you there." Eli, who knew his way around her kitchen as well as she did at this point, added forks, knives, and napkins to the pile. "Why don't I have a key to your place?"

"We can talk about that later. Right now, we've got bigger problems." She shoveled some *pad woon sen* onto her plate. "Did you see the surveyor's flags outside?"

"No." A flicker of something she couldn't quite identify crossed Eli's face, only to be quickly replaced by a blank, neutral mask. "I was in a hurry to get the food upstairs before it got cold."

"So much better than mac and cheese," David, seated on the sofa with his plate balanced on his knees, muttered through a mouthful of drunken noodles.

"A survey means the building's been sold, right?" Brooke finished loading up her plate and took the chair across from David.

"And the new owner's going to knock it down," David added. "Or convert the units into condos and throw us all out on our asses."

"Not necessarily." Eli's speech was hesitant, his tone strangely evasive. He averted his eyes as he sat on the far end of the couch from David, developing a sudden fascination with his *panang gai*. "They could still be in negotiations. And a new owner's probably going to want a survey even if he doesn't plan on making major changes."

David gave Eli a side-eye glance. "You sound like you know what you're talking about."

Eli continued his preoccupation with his chicken curry. Strange, since he didn't seem to be eating much of it, just pushing it around on his plate. "I've got some friends in real estate."

"Maybe you could ask around, see if they've heard anything," Brooke suggested, her voice a touch more panicked than she'd intended. She was already freaked out by the little flags all over the place. Despite his reassuring words, Eli's odd behavior wasn't helping any. "We tried talking to the surveyor, but he either didn't have any information or didn't want to share it."

"Uh, sure." Eli lifted a forkful of food to his mouth. Finally. "No problem."

His cell chimed. He set his plate down on the coffee table and pulled the phone out of his pocket, frowning as he studied the screen.

"Something wrong?" Brooke asked.

"Shit," he hissed, still scowling at his phone.

"I take it that's a yes," David observed wryly.

"Work crisis." Eli shoved the phone back in his pocket and stood, bumping the coffee table and almost knocking his still full plate onto the floor. He caught it just in time and brought it into the kitchen. "I'm sorry, I have to go deal with this."

"Now?" Brooke got up and followed him.

"It can't wait." He grabbed his coat from the back of the couch, shoved his arms through the sleeves and gave her a quick, distracted kiss. "I'll text you later."

She watched him disappear out the door then turned back to David, who was scraping up the last of his drunken noodles.

"What do we do now?" David asked. "About Candy Court?"

Brooke dumped the rest of her *pad woon sen* in the garbage and put her plate in the sink, her appetite suddenly gone. "We make flyers."

"Flyers?" David looked at her blankly, his jaw slack.

"Advertising a neighborhood meeting." She sat down at her drafting table and ripped a fresh sheet of paper off her sketchpad. "Then we post them in all the local businesses. There's strength in numbers. If the new owner thinks he's going to march in here and turn this place into some sort of yuppie, hipster paradise, we're going to be ready for him. And we're not going down without a fight."

Chapter Twelve

"Eli." Simon greeted him at his office door. "You're looking well rested. How was Tibet? I wanted to contact you, but Ginny said you needed some time away from everything to..."

"Fuck Tibet." Eli pushed his way past his former friend and business partner and threw a folder down on his desk. It had been burning a hole through his hands ever since Ginny gave it to him, about an hour after he'd gotten her text message. His next move was a terse call to Simon, asking to meet him at Momentum, well past business hours, when no one else was around to eavesdrop on what was sure to be an unpleasant conversation. And that was putting it mildly. "What the hell is this?"

Simon followed Eli into the room and took a seat in the high-backed leather chair behind his equally impressive mahogany desk. Unlike Eli's office, which was all sleek glass and polished steel, Simon had gone for rich leather and dark wood, giving the room a traditional, sophisticated feel. He flipped the folder open, his face blanching as he leafed through the contents.

"I don't understand." He ran a hand through his close-cropped blond hair.

"That makes two of us." Eli sat in one of the two only slightly smaller, less imposing guest chairs.

Simon pinched the bridge of his nose. "How did you get these?"

"That's not important." Eli wasn't about to get sidetracked. He reached across the desk and jabbed a finger at the picture on top of the pile, which showed Krystal, the eager, young, and, not coincidentally, attractive PA Simon had hired not six months ago, sitting with Noel Dupree at what looked like a Starbucks. An eight by ten manila envelope, fat with papers, sat on the table between them. "Why is your PA meeting with our biggest competitor, the man who beat us to the punch on our last four projects?"

Simon slammed the folder shut and slumped in his chair, his face now drawn as well as pale. "I have no idea."

Eli leaned forward, elbows on his knees. "You seriously expect me to believe you had nothing to do with this? I've suspected you were working with Dupree since we lost the East Harlem building. You and I were the only ones who knew about that project."

Simon's hands went limp. "And that's why you took off for Tibet?"

"I wasn't in Tibet." Eli didn't elaborate, just sat with his jaw clenched and his hands folded in his lap until Simon broke the silence.

"Momentum is mine, too. We built it together. Why would I do anything to jeopardize that?"

"I don't know." Eli fixed him with a hard, piercing glare. "You tell me."

Simon's jaw was set, his tone insistent. "I wouldn't. Not intentionally."

"What do you mean, 'not intentionally'?" Eli scoffed.

"I might have let something slip to Krystal." Simon buried his head in his hands. His voice was muffled and small. "In bed."

"You're fucking her?" Eli swore under his breath. How could his partner be so stupid? "I thought we agreed. No dipping our wicks in the company ink."

"Was. She dumped me last week." Simon lifted his head. He looked at bad as Eli felt. The dilated pupils. The sweaty palms. The labored breathing. Either the guy was having a heart attack, or he was telling the truth about Krystal. "Not my finest moment, I know. I let my dick do the thinking, and I'm sorry."

"Been there, done that, bought the T-shirt and wore it out." Eli let out a short, scornful laugh. But his words were flat, devoid of anger. Instead, looking at Simon, he felt nothing but pity and a strange sense of understanding. Hadn't he had sex with Brooke hours after meeting her? Of course, their relationship had progressed way past a casual hookup, but he had no way of knowing where they were headed when he screwed her sideways on a futon in the back room of a dive bar. He steepled his fingers over his chest and refocused on the reason for his visit. "But I'm not here to talk about your love life. Or mine. I'm here to find out what the fuck your assistant's doing with Dupree."

"I told you, I didn't have anything to do with that." Simon sighed and rubbed the back of his neck. "It's as much a surprise to me as it is to you."

Eli tilted his head. "Give me one reason why I should believe you."

"I can't." Simon seemed to sink farther into his chair, his posture screaming defeat. "Except that I have as much invested in Momentum as you do. Selling out to Dupree would be entirely against my self-interest."

He had a point there, one that hadn't escaped Eli. But that left one huge, unanswered question. "Why would Krystal do this on her own?"

"I don't know." Simon's eyebrows pulled together. "But now that I think of it, she has been a little off lately."

Eli smirked, remembering the last time he'd seen his partner's assistant, sitting at her desk, filing her nails. She hadn't even bothered to look up at him when he'd asked to see Simon. "With her, how can you tell?"

Simon reopened the folder and flipped through the pictures. "These are good. How did you get them?"

"I've had a PI following Dupree for a few weeks."

"Smart move." Simon picked up a pen and twirled it between his fingers. "But we're going to need more evidence to prove Krystal violated her non-disclosure agreement."

Eli leaned back in his chair and crossed an ankle over one knee. "What do you mean 'we'?"

"I have no right to ask you this, but I'm going to anyway. Give me two weeks." Simon stood and came around to sit on the corner of his desk. "I'll get what we need to nab Krystal. I promise. And in the meantime, I'll make sure she doesn't have access to any more sensitive information."

"How are you going to do that?" Eli asked.

"Plant a dummy file. Then when Dupree starts sniffing around, we'll know exactly where his information came from."

As much as he didn't want to, Eli had to admit it wasn't a half bad idea. And one a guilty person would never have suggested in a million years. "You really didn't put Krystal up to this, did you?"

"No." Simon jutted out his chin. "I didn't."

Eli studied his friend for a long minute before speaking. When he did, he weighed his words carefully. "I can help create the fake file."

"Does that mean you're coming back to work? Ginny's

done a great job covering for you, but I miss my partner." Simon's voice broke, and he stared down at his hands. "I miss my friend."

Eli swallowed a lump in his throat. He hadn't expected to feel sympathy for Simon. When he'd walked through the door to his partner's office, he'd come in with guns blazing, his only thought retribution, his only emotion white-hot anger.

But that anger had quickly dissipated. What was the point in being mad at someone who was so clearly miserable? Besides, if it weren't for Simon shooting his mouth off to Krystal and torpedoing the East Harlem deal, Eli would never have met Brooke. That didn't mean Eli was ready to forgive him. But maybe he could forget long enough for them to catch Krystal.

"Not yet." Possibly not ever. Even if he managed to look past his best friend's lapse in judgment for the sake of smoking out their mole, Eli wasn't sure he could ever trust Simon again. And trust was essential in a business partnership. "I've got some things to wrap up in Brooklyn."

"Brooklyn?" Simon blinked. "So that's where you've been hiding."

Eli ignored his comment and stood. "We can collaborate remotely, through our private emails. And Ginny. I tell her everything."

"Everything?" Simon's Adam's apple bobbed up and down in his throat.

"Don't worry," Eli assured him. "I won't say anything about you and Krystal. Your private life is just that. Private."

Simon let out a relieved sigh. "I appreciate that."

"I'm not doing it for you. I'm doing it for Ginny. For some strange reason, she thinks you walk on water. I'd hate to see her disillusioned." Eli moved toward the door. There wasn't anything left to be said between them, not tonight. Now he wanted to get back to Brooklyn. Back to Brooke.

"I appreciate it anyway." Simon rose and followed him. "Will you be at the silent auction on Saturday?"

Damn. With all the shit going on in his fucked-up life, the Geek Girls benefit kept slipping his mind. He made a mental note to have Ginny send him a day-of reminder. If he was smart, he'd head into the city on Friday and spend a couple of nights at the penthouse. Although that meant two long, lonely nights in his California king without Brooke. "Of course. Paige would have my head on a platter if I missed it."

"As a board member, I was planning on attending, but if you'd rather I not..."

"It's fine," Eli said, cutting him off. "I'm good with it if you are."

"Thanks." They reached the door. Simon opened it and stuck out his hand awkwardly. "For not being half the asshole I would have been if our positions were reversed."

Eli probably would have been twice the asshole if it weren't for Brooke. It was hard to be pissed about losing something when you'd gained so much more.

Still, he wasn't ready to bury the hatchet just yet. "There's still plenty of time for that." He ignored his friend's hand and stepped past him into the corridor, his feet pointed automatically toward the elevator bank at the end of the hall. "First, we've got a huge-ass fire to put out."

• • •

Brooke was halfway to dreamland, images of her and Eli in a variety of increasingly interesting sexual positions flickering behind her closed eyes like a hard-core porn highlight reel, when a knock so soft she almost didn't hear it interrupted the movie in her mind. She sat up and listened again.

Three knocks. Louder this time.

She threw off her blankets, padded across the loft in her

thick, fuzzy socks, and peered through the peephole. Eli stood on the other side, wearing the same clothes he'd rushed off in hours earlier.

"So now you knock?" she joked, opening the door and stepping back to let him in.

"See?" He wrapped one arm around her waist and lifted her off her feet, simultaneously kicking the door shut and bringing her mouth level with his. "They were wrong. You can teach an old dog new tricks."

She breathed in the scent of him, warm and soapy, with a hint of his citrusy cologne. Her fingers tangled in the silky, dark hair at the nape of his neck. "Is everything okay?"

"It is now." He crushed his lips to hers and took possession, his free hand coming up to hold her head in place for a deep, brutal kiss. She was sinking, drowning in him. Seemingly of their own volition, her legs circled his waist, pulling him imperceptibly closer.

"Do you want to talk about it?" she asked, her voice husky with lust when he finally let her up for air.

"Talk about what?"

"Whatever you're avoiding talking about by kissing me."

"Can't I kiss you for the sake of kissing you?" As if to prove his point, he lowered his mouth to the hollow where her neck met the curve of her shoulder, leaving a trail of hot, wet kisses along her collarbone.

"Of course." She arched away from him, and he lifted his head to meet her gaze. "But I can tell the difference between a kiss for the sake of kissing and a kiss for the sake of avoiding."

"We'll talk later." His eyes drifted downward, lingering on her vintage Rainbow Brite T-shirt and hot-pink flannel pajama pants. "First I want to get you out of these and under me."

"You don't approve of my taste in sleepwear?"

"You could be wearing a gunnysack and granny panties,

and I'd still want you."

Okay, so he didn't want to talk. Talking was overrated anyway, and they had all night for that.

In two long strides, he crossed the floor to the bed. All Brooke could do was hold on for dear life until he laid her down and stretched out beside her. His fingers latched onto the waistband of her sleep pants, and she instinctively lifted her hips so he could slide them off. Her shirt went next, landing next to her pants on the floor beside the bed.

She reached up to grab the lapels of his overcoat, which he hadn't bothered to remove in his haste to get her in the sack. "Why don't you take your coat off and stay a while?"

"Don't mind if I do."

He rolled away from her and stood, shedding not only his coat but the rest of his clothes and rejoining her on the bed before she had a chance to miss his warmth. He didn't waste any time getting back to business, either, zeroing in on her breasts with his hands, teasing her nipples into hard little points.

Only when they were practically screaming for more did his mouth get in on the action. He latched on to one stiff peak and suckled, then licked, then bit, each new sensation made all the more delicious by the sensual scraping of his beard against her sensitive skin.

One hand snaked down to the wet, pulsing heat between her thighs. "Open."

She obeyed—like there was really any question—and let her legs fall apart. One gentle probe with his finger told him she was slick and ready for him. Within seconds, he was inside her, the weight of him pressing her into the mattress, solid and good and right. There was nothing patient or gentle or careful about this pairing. It was raw, primal, end-of-the-world-as-we-know-it sex. The universe narrowed to him, her, the place where their bodies were joined, and the heavenly friction between her thighs.

She spurred him on, her nails digging little half-moons in his shoulders and back. Her body was like a rocket on the launchpad, primed and ready to shoot off. It didn't take much to send her into orbit. Waves of pleasure rippled through her, triggering Eli's release.

He collapsed beside her, their bodies still fused together. They lay there in silence, satisfied and sweaty, the only noises the sound of their breathing and the distant rumble of cars and voices from the street below. Her thoughts spun in circles. Each time she and Eli were together was more powerfully mind-numbing than the last. Each time she gave a little more of herself. More of her trust. More of her heart. More of her soul.

Had she done the unimaginable? Had she given herself over completely to him?

She shifted, pulling them apart.

Eli looked down and his muscles tensed. The fingers of one hand clenched and unclenched spasmodically. "Shit."

Her eyes followed his gaze to where they'd been joined. It wasn't what she saw there but what she didn't see that made her understand his strange reaction.

No condom.

"Shit," he repeated. His hand balled into a fist, and he punched the mattress. "I can't believe I forgot to suit up."

"I can. You were like a man possessed." He hit the mattress again, harder this time. She took his face in her hands, tilting it upward so he was forced to look her in the eyes, and smoothed a stray lock of hair off his brow. "It's okay. We both got carried away. Besides, I'm on the pill. And I haven't been with anyone else in… Well, let's just say it's been a while."

The tension leaked from his body like air from a punctured tire. "Same here. I mean, I'm clean."

"Then we're good?" She drew back to study him.

His deep, masculine chuckle warmed her from her toes up. "Yeah, we're good."

He rolled onto his back and gathered her close, throwing one leg across her hips to make sure they stayed that way. "There's something I need to talk to you about."

The dreaded we-have-to-talk. Brooke's heart squeezed into a knot, and her stomach plummeted what seemed like twenty stories. She fought to keep her tone light and her thoughts positive. "That sounds ominous. Do you have a wife and kids stashed somewhere? Are you on the FBI's most wanted list?"

He laughed softly and kissed her nose. "Nothing that dire. I've got to go away for a couple of days. Business."

"Is that all?" Relief coursed through her like a sugar rush. "We're not joined at the hip, you know."

"Could have fooled me." His leg pressed into the small of her back, pulling her tight to him. "Not that I'm complaining."

"How long will you be gone?"

"I'm leaving tomorrow, but I should be back sometime Sunday afternoon."

"As luck would have it, I won't be here this weekend, either." She made a face. "Family stuff."

"You don't seem too excited."

"I'm not." Going to some hoity-toity fundraiser at the Worthington wasn't exactly her idea of a rockin' good time. "But I promised my sister I'd be there. I owe her for helping with the wedding."

"Do you think you can manage two whole days without me?" His breath was hot against her ear, making her shiver.

"It'll be hard, but I'll try."

He ground his hips against her, rubbing his already stiffening cock against her thigh. "Oh, it'll be hard all right."

Her traitorous body responded, her nipples hardening and a tingling sensation vibrating between her legs. "Is that all you think about?"

"When you're lying in my arms naked?" He took one finger and drew a sensuous line from her neck to the valley between her breasts. "Hell, yes. It's pretty much impossible to think about anything else."

She couldn't argue with that. She had the same problem where he was concerned.

"I'm flattered." She shuddered as she sucked in a breath. "I think."

"What do you say?" His wandering finger found her nipple. "One more round to tide us over until Sunday?"

She closed her eyes and surrendered to the waves of pleasure that took hold of her body whenever Eli touched her. "At least."

Chapter Thirteen

The ballroom at the Park Avenue Worthington was just about the last place Brooke wanted to be on a Saturday night—or any night, for that matter—but she had to admit the staff had gone all out. The room was ringed with long, black-skirted tables. More tables formed a square at the center of the room. Each one held an array of items from bottles of wine to Yankees tickets to gift certificates for some of Manhattan's most exclusive restaurants, all up for bid. Rumor had it a walk-on part in a Broadway play was up for grabs.

Smartly dressed waitstaff circulated among the growing crowd with trays of mouth-watering hors d'oeuvres and glasses of champagne and sparkling water. At the far end of the room, a stage was set up with a podium and microphone. Balloon bouquets and floral arrangements dotted the room, adding pops of color.

"Wow." She turned to her sister, who looked stunning in a black sleeveless Valentino cocktail dress and matching patent leather Louboutins. Brooke felt dowdy in comparison in the tomato-red fit-and-flare number she'd pulled off the clearance rack at Neiman Marcus. She smoothed down the skirt, wishing she were home in her yoga pants and an extra-large T-shirt. Or better yet, buck naked in bed with Eli. "You've really outdone yourself."

Mallory waved off the compliment with a perfectly manicured hand. "I'm the chef. I'm only responsible for the food."

"You can't fool me." Brooke snagged a glass of champagne from a passing waiter. "This thing has your fingerprints all over it."

"Well, I did collaborate with the event planner," Mallory confessed, blushing and taking a sip of her sparkling water. Her sister had never been very good at accepting praise.

Brooke decided to let her off the hook and change the subject. "Dare I ask about the whereabouts of dear old Mom and Dad?"

"They're around here somewhere." A man in a white coat flagged Mallory down from across the room. She acknowledged him with a nod and handed Brooke her glass. "That's my sous chef. Must be some minor emergency in the kitchen. I'll be back as soon as I can."

Brooke spent the next half hour meandering around the ballroom, making small talk with strangers and family friends she barely remembered and checking out all the items up for auction. Signed sports memorabilia. Exotic vacations. Golf lessons. She was scrawling her signature on one of the bid sheets when her mother's piercing, judgmental voice stopped her pen midstroke.

"A hot air balloon ride, Brooke? Really? Do you think that's practical?"

"No, Mom, I don't." Brooke finished signing with a flourish and turned to face her mother. No surprise, she was decked out to the nines in a floor-length beaded gown, her makeup flawless, not a frosted white-blond hair out of place.

"But I think it sounds like fun. And it's for a good cause."

She assumed. To be honest, she hadn't paid much attention to the cause célèbre du jour. If memory served, the signs at the entrance to the ballroom said something about girls and science. A refreshing change from saving whales or building houses or fighting disease. Not that there was anything wrong with saving whales or building houses or fighting disease.

"Where's your young man?" her mother asked, one plucked eyebrow inching upward.

"Not here." Brooke didn't volunteer more.

Her mother's eyebrow rose higher, disappearing beneath her frosted bangs, but she didn't press. "Well, at least you made it."

"Brooke." Her father joined them, putting an arm around his wife, whether for show or because there was still some real affection between them Brooke was never sure. "You look lovely."

"Yes." Her mother looked her up and down, her expression shockingly more supportive than scornful. "That color suits you."

"Um, thanks." Compliments were so rare from her parents, Brooke didn't quite know how to react. Fortunately, a tall, blond-haired man who was a close second to Eli in the heart-stoppingly gorgeous department stepped onto the stage and tapped the microphone, diverting their attention.

"Hello and welcome. I'm Simon Adler, and on behalf of the board of directors of Geek Girls, I'd like to thank each and every one of you for coming out tonight."

The crowd applauded politely, and he continued. "I hope you brought your checkbooks because we've got all sorts of great items up for auction. So remember, bid often and bid high."

Laughter. When it died down, Simon went on with his speech. "In a few minutes, you'll be hearing from our board president, who'll let you in on some exciting things we have planned for this year, but until then eat, drink, and of course, bid."

The crowd applauded again, a little more enthusiastically this time, and Simon left the stage. Gradually, the hum of conversation and the clinking of glassware resurged, filling the ballroom.

"Richard." Never Rich. And certainly not Dick. Her mother was nothing if not predictable. She laid a bony, ringed hand on her husband's arm and with the other gestured to a couple on the other side of the room. "I think I see the Garrisons. We should say hello."

"Yes." Her father nodded to Brooke as his wife dragged him away. "We'll catch up with you later."

Not if I see you first. "Sure thing."

Brooke hijacked another waiter, handed off Mallory's half-full sparkling water and exchanged her now empty champagne glass for a fresh one. She sipped and scanned the ballroom for her sister, coming up empty. The emergency in the kitchen must be proving more major than minor.

Just when she was about to give up hope and hit the bar for something stronger than champagne, Mallory showed up.

"Everything okay?" Brooke asked.

"It is now." Her sister stopped a waitress, took a canapé from the tray she was bearing, and bit into it. "Tell Hector it needs more mascarpone."

The waitress nodded and hurried off.

"Did you find Mom and Dad?" Mallory popped the rest of the canapé into her mouth.

"More like they found me," Brooke grumbled.

"Let me guess. Mom wanted to know why your young man isn't here," Mallory said, putting air quotes around "young man."

Brooke let out an unladylike snort. "How did you know?"

"She grilled me about Hunter."

"Where is the boy wonder tonight?"

"He's on call." Mallory's ever-present smile slipped a little. "And I wish you wouldn't call him that."

A pang of guilt sucker-punched Brooke in the gut. She'd been so busy with Eli and the wedding she'd never had a chance to talk to her sister about Hunter. More like never made the time, she scolded herself, remembering how she'd canceled their lunch date after the wedding.

The guilt doubled, then tripled.

"I'm sorry. I'm sure Hunter's a great guy." Brooke tried her hardest to sound convincing. "It's just…"

The lights flickered, and Mallory put a finger to her lips. "Shh. They're about to start."

Simon Adler returned to the stage, this time accompanied by a slightly taller man with cerulean-blue eyes and dark hair that curled over the collar of his tuxedo.

Eyes that had seen every inch of Brooke's body. Hair her fingers knew the silky feel of almost as well as her own.

Mallory clutched her sister's arm in a death grip. "Isn't that…"

"Yes," Brooke ground out between clenched teeth. "It is."

"I take it you didn't know he'd be here."

"No." Brooke watched him step up to the podium, a vein pulsing in her temple. "I have no clue what he's doing here or why."

"Good evening." He flashed the crowd a disarming smile she was more than well acquainted with. "I'm Eli Ward, president of the Geek Girls board of directors and co-founder of Momentum Development, the sponsor of this evening's event."

What. The actual. Fuck.

Anger warred with heartbreak as Brooke tried to process what she was seeing. Her Eli Ward was *the* Eli Ward, the one her parents had talked about at brunch. Billionaire real estate developer. One of *Fortune's* most influential businesspeople under forty, or some crap like that.

If he'd ever been hers at all.

She considered turning tail and running. Almost as quickly as the thought popped into her head, she rejected it. She'd always been more of a fight than flight kind of gal. And her need to know why Eli had been lying to her all this time trumped her desire to bury her sorrows in a pint of Ben & Jerry's Chunky Monkey.

"I don't have a clue," Brooke repeated, shaking off her sister's hand and lowering her voice to a hard, cold whisper. "But I'm sure as hell going to find out."

• • •

The night was going perfectly according to plan. Beautiful ballroom. Good food. Free-flowing alcohol. And tons of eager bidders. By Eli's estimate, Geek Girls should have an additional hundred grand, minimum, in its coffers by the end of the evening.

He'd finished his speech and was barely off the stage when his sister intercepted him, steering him into a corner away from the tables of auction merchandise. "Houston, we have a problem."

Great. More mess.

Eli glanced around the room. Still nothing but happy campers as far as he could see. "What's wrong? Seems like everything is going great."

"Pissed-off brunette at eleven o'clock," Paige hissed. "Says she needs to talk to you and only you."

He frowned. "Why me? What does she want?"

"Who knows? She didn't say." Paige looked over her shoulder and swore under her breath. "I was hoping to hustle you out of here, but she's on her way over. I hope you can diffuse this without creating a scene."

"Trust me. Whatever it is, I'll take care of…"

The words curled up in his throat and died when he caught site of the woman storming her way across the room. In other circumstances, he'd be admiring her long legs in her open-toed stilettos, the way her fire-engine-red dress clung to her breasts and hugged her tiny waist before flaring out at her hips. Now all he could focus on was the murderous glint in her eyes and the steam practically coming out of her ears.

"Told you she was pissed," his sister warned as Brooke bore down on them. "Is she one of your exes or something? Are you sure you didn't break her heart?"

No, he wasn't. But she might be about to break his.

He acknowledged what he'd been shoving to the back of his brain for weeks. He was in love with Brooke. Why else would he barely bat an eyelash when Simon confessed to having a fling with his PA? Why else would he do a complete one-eighty on his plans for Candy Court?

And now he was going to lose her, unless he could convince her that he wasn't a complete douchebag for lying to her.

"I'm out of here," Paige said, turning on her heel and sprinting for the door just as Brooke was about to reach them.

"Good luck, big brother," she called over her shoulder. "Remember, no ugly scenes. It's bad for business."

"Thanks for nothing," Eli muttered at her retreating back. But Paige was right. He didn't need her as backup. This was something only he could fix.

"This was what you meant by 'I'm in finance.'" Brooke stood in front of him, fists on her hips, feet firmly planted at least twelve inches apart. Her Wonder Woman power pose, reserved for when she was really fuming. Like now. "According to my parents, you're some sort of hotshot real estate mogul. And here I was picturing you bent over a calculator, crunching numbers."

He scrubbed a hand across his freshly shaven jaw. "We need to talk."

"No shit, Sherlock."

His eyes flicked around the jam-packed ballroom. Way too many witnesses within earshot. "But not here."

"What's wrong with here?" She waved a hand wildly. "I've got nothing to hide."

"You might not. But I do." He reached out to put a hand on her shoulder, but she flinched and pulled away. "Please. I promised my sister we wouldn't make a scene. Geek Girls was our parents' brainchild. It's really important to her."

And to him. But not half as important as Brooke.

She huffed out an exasperated breath. "Fine. But not for you. For your sister. And because it's for charity."

He didn't dare try to touch her again, so he motioned for her to follow him into the hallway. He took a sharp left, heading away from the hotel lobby and the overflow crowd gathered there, and opened the first door he came to, which turned out to be a supply closet.

"In here." He stood back and held the door for her to precede him.

"Are you serious?" She peered in at the shelves of toilet paper, soaps, and cleaners. "You realize this is a closet, right?"

He leaned against the open door. "Which pretty much guarantees we won't be interrupted."

"If it means we can get this over with, then I'll go." She pushed past him. "But don't blame me if it's a little cramped."

Get this over with. Didn't sound promising, but he hadn't made *Fortune* magazine by giving up when the going got tough. There was one, big difference, though. This wasn't some cold, impersonal business transaction. This was his future. This was Brooke.

He wiped his damp hands on his tuxedo pants and followed her into the closet. Brooke stood with her back to him, her shoulders pinched together.

"Let's have it," she said without turning around. "I can't wait to hear your excuse for letting me believe you were a normal guy."

"I am a normal guy," he insisted.

She turned to face him. "You know what I mean."

"I never set out to lie to you." Lame, he knew. But he had to start somewhere.

"But you did." She braced herself against one of the shelves, knocking a roll of toilet paper to the floor. "Did you get a kick out of slumming? Seducing the poor, lonely bartender?"

"As I recall, the seduction was mutual. And neither one of us was interested in exchanging personal information."

"I'll give you that. But you've had almost three months to tell me who you are. Was it some sort of game, seeing how long you could keep me in the dark?"

"No. It wasn't anything like that. That night at the bar…" He scraped a hand through his hair, debating how much he should reveal. Fuck it. Enough holding back. Time for the truth. The whole truth, no matter how personal or embarrassing. "I'd just found out someone was leaking information to Momentum's biggest competitor. And the prime suspect was my business partner."

"The guy on stage with you?"

"One and the same. He also happens—or happened—to be my best friend."

"Ouch." She crossed her arms in front of her chest. "Sucks to be you."

He ignored the dig. Hell, he deserved that and worse. "Which explains why I decided to lay low for a while in Brooklyn. I needed time to gather evidence. Uncover the mole before he—or she—did any more damage."

"But it doesn't explain why you had to lie to me." Was he imagining things, or had her voice lost a little of its harshness? "I would have kept your secret."

"I know. It wasn't that I didn't trust you."

"Then what?"

He loosened his bow tie, struggling to find the right words. "I guess I just liked being Eli Ward, average Joe. Liked knowing you wanted me for me, not…"

"Your money?" she finished for him.

"Who I was—no, who I am—with you, that guy is a thousand times more authentic than the one you saw up on stage tonight. With you, I can let down my guard and just… be. That's pretty rare for me, almost nonexistent. I didn't want to lose it."

She stared at him, silent, so he kept going, hoping against hope that he was making some headway. "Once we got involved, I wanted to tell you the truth, but it never seemed to be the right time."

"It must be hard never knowing if someone's with you for you or what you can do for them." She kicked off one shoe and wiggled her toes, flashing her brightly painted nails. Not fire-engine-red to match her dress, like most women would have chosen, but an electric purple. Totally unexpected. Totally Brooke.

"Yeah." He let out a short, harsh laugh. "Poor little rich boy."

"That's not what I meant." She slipped her foot back into her shoe and stood tall. "I have something to tell you, too."

"Wait." He held up a hand. "I'm not done."

She sucked her bottom lip between her teeth. "You don't understand…"

"Please," he interrupted, his voice dripping with desperation. "If I don't say this now, it will be too late."

"Too late for what?" She looked at him side-eyed. "Don't tell me. You witnessed a mob hit, and you're going into the witness protection program."

"Not exactly." His fingers curled and uncurled nervously at his sides. Brooke wouldn't be making wisecracks when she heard what was coming next. "But you might want to ship me off somewhere when you find out what it is."

"How much worse could it be than hiding your identity?"

Way worse. "You know there's an offer out on Candy Court."

"Of course." She rolled her eyes at him like he was Captain Obvious. "The surveyor was there the other day, remember? We're having a neighborhood meeting at the end of the month to formulate our response. There's no way some opportunistic asshole bent on gentrification is going to come in and kick us out of our homes without a fight."

The vehemence in her last sentence made the knot in his stomach seize up, but he forged on. No turning back now. Come hell or high water, this closet was going to be his confessional. He just hoped Brooke was willing to absolve him from his sins. "The asshole is me."

Time seemed to freeze, the closet eerily quiet except for the sound of their shallow breaths. It could have been ten seconds or ten hours before she spoke. "What do you mean?"

"I mean I'm the one buying Candy Court. My company, that is. The Hearthstone Group."

"No." She shook her head, distracting him with waves of coconut and citrus from her shampoo. *Focus man, focus.* "I heard you up there on that stage. Your company is called Momentum Development."

"One of my companies. Hearthstone is another."

"Let me get this straight." Brooke tapped one toe on the tile floor. "You own Hearthstone."

"Right."

"And Hearthstone is buying Candy Court."

"Right." He folded his arms across his chest then stuffed his hands in his pockets then let them fall to his sides, uncertain of how to stand or what to say. He was fucking this up, damn it, and he didn't know how to fix it. "But…"

"How long?" she asked, cutting him off sharply.

"What?"

She took a step toward him in their already tight quarters, eyes blazing. The Wonder Woman power pose was back, not that he blamed her. "How long have you been planning this? From the night we met at Flotsam and Jetsam? The day you walked into the tenants' meeting?"

The guilty-as-charged look on his face must have given her the answer because her eyes went from hot with fury to ice cold and her lips flattened into a hard slash across her face. "You bastard."

"I…"

"You were one of us. We accepted you, no questions asked. Hell, David and Chris had you in their wedding. Mrs. Feingold treats you like a son. And I…" Her voice caught, and she blinked back tears. "I fell in love with you. And the whole time you've not only been lying about who you are, which I could understand and maybe even forgive given the circumstances, you've been secretly plotting to buy our building out from under us and throw us out on the street."

His heart twisted like she'd plunged in a knife. A long, rusty knife with serrated edges that continued to rip and tear with every breath he took.

"It's not like that." He reached out a hand to her, but she smacked it away. The knife plunged deeper. "Please. Listen to me. Wait until you hear what I have planned…"

"I don't care about your plans. There's not one damn thing you can say that will make any difference." She pushed past him and jerked open the door. "Fuck you, Eli Ward, and the D-train you rode in on. I'll see you in court."

She stormed out, leaving Eli standing among the cleaning supplies and toiletries. Numbly, he bent to pick up the roll of toilet paper she'd knocked over. Only then did it hit him.

She'd said she loved him.

Chapter Fourteen

"Get out," Eli barked, slamming shut the file he'd been reviewing. He shoved it across his desk at the hapless flunky who'd no doubt drawn the short straw and been sent into the lion's den. Eli didn't know his name, and to be honest, he didn't give a shit. Just like he hadn't given a shit about anything in the two weeks since Brooke had stranded him in the storage closet. "And don't come back until those numbers are right. Check them as many times as it takes to be sure."

"Y-yes, sir," the flunky stammered, picking up the file and backing toward the door.

"I need them on my desk first thing in the morning. I don't care if it means you're here all night."

"Yes, sir."

He fled as fast as his shiny shoes would take him. Eli opened another file and tried to focus, but the numbers and letters swam in front of him.

"Heard you scared off another one," Simon observed, coming into the office without knocking. "Keep it up and we won't have any associates left. At least, none willing to work with you."

"Don't you ever knock?" Even as he said the words, Eli heard them in Brooke's voice, giving him hell for his habit of entering unannounced. The knife that had been lodged in his heart for the past fourteen days twisted again.

"Nope." Simon took up residence in one of Eli's guest chairs, stretched out his long legs, and crossed them at the ankles. "Partner privilege."

Eli leaned back in his chair and studied the man who had been his friend since college. He'd struggled with whether to continue their partnership. His original intention had been to leave Momentum and force Simon to buy him out and waive their non-compete agreement so Eli could throw all of his energy into Hearthstone. But somehow, with Brooke out of the picture, that didn't seem quite as appealing now.

So he'd decided not to make any rash moves, at least until they'd outed Krystal as their mole and gotten Momentum back on track. That had all come to a head yesterday when she brought Dupree a copy of the dummy file Simon planted. It hadn't taken long for Dupree to take the bait and call Ginny, who was posing as the commercial real estate broker handling the fictitious transaction.

Simon propped his feet up on Eli's desk. "You look like shit."

Eli looked down at his outfit. Immaculately tailored gray herringbone suit. Pale blue button-down shirt. Navy polka-dot tie. Now that he was back in the penthouse, he had his full wardrobe at his disposal. Small compensation for losing the woman he loved. "This is my favorite suit. And I'm pretty sure you gave me the tie."

"I'm not talking about your goddamn clothes. I'm talking about the circles under your eyes. Are you sleeping?"

"Yes." If an hour a night—two, tops—counted as sleep. Eli did a quick reverse and changed the subject. "How did it go with Krystal? She out?"

"She was escorted from the building half an hour ago without incident." Simon laced his fingers together. "I've turned everything over to the police. They'll let us know if there's enough to prosecute."

"Glad that's taken care of that." Eli stood, took off his jacket, and hung it on the hanger behind his door. Then he crossed to his credenza where he uncorked a decanter of Macallan Sherry Oak and poured out generous amounts of the amber liquid in two glasses. "Any idea why she sold us out?"

He handed one glass to Simon, who took it and sipped before answering. "Money. Turns out she was doing more than her nails at her desk. She was a compulsive online shopper. All her credit cards were maxed out, and she was three months behind in rent. Dupree paid her ten grand for every tip and promised her a job down the line."

"Ten grand," Eli scoffed. He sat on the edge of his desk and pushed Simon's feet off. "That's chump change for him. Cheapskate."

They drank in silence for a minute before Simon spoke. "Now that all this shit with Krystal and Dupree is in the rearview mirror, I have to ask. Are we good?"

"Truth?"

"Truth."

Eli swirled his scotch. "I don't know if we'll ever be good. I'm hoping our business relationship can be saved. But you slept with your PA. Risked everything we spent years building together. I'm not going to be able to forget that any time soon."

"I thought I was in love with her." Simon slumped in his seat and took a healthy slug of scotch. "I don't know how it happened, or why. But once it started, it was like I was powerless to stop it."

"The heart wants what it wants." Eli swirled and sipped, swirled, and sipped again. "There's no denying it."

"Sounds like you're speaking from experience."

"What makes you think that?"

Simon absentmindedly ran a finger around the rim of his glass as he studied Eli. "Why else would you be stomping around here like Godzilla?"

"Are you seriously expecting me to discuss my love life with you?"

"Does it have anything to do with Brooke Worthington?"

It was a good thing Eli had a tight grasp on his glass or it would have hit the floor. "How do you know about Brooke?"

"Paige said she was looking for you at the auction, and I saw the two of you leave together."

"Well if you saw us leave together, then you know it wasn't all sunshine and roses." Eli drained his glass and strode over to the credenza to get a refill. This was definitely a two-scotch conversation. Maybe three.

"What did you do to piss off the hotel heiress?"

Eli's palms started to sweat. He wiped them on his pants and somehow managed to pour two fingers of scotch without sloshing it all over the floor. "The what?"

"Brooke Worthington. Heir apparent to the Worthington hotel chain." Simon gaped at him. "You didn't know?"

Worthington. Why hadn't he made the connection? Probably for the same reason he'd been able to fly under the radar on the other side of the Brooklyn Bridge. He wasn't expecting to find a hotel heiress in Sunset Park. And like him, Brooke hadn't wanted to make a big deal out of her wealth. Okay, so she hadn't out-and-out lied about it like he had, but she hadn't exactly been forthcoming, either. No wonder she'd been so understanding about that part of his deception. Too bad he had to compound it by hiding the fact that he was going to be her new landlord.

Eli settled back behind his desk with his drink. "Can't say I blame her for keeping it to herself. It's not like I was entirely truthful with her."

"Hold on." Simon held up a hand. "You lost me. Back up and start at the beginning."

Maybe it was the scotch. Maybe it was the fact that Simon had been his closest friend for over ten years. Whatever the reason, Eli found himself giving him the condensed version of his relationship with Brooke, concluding with the whole sorry scene in the closet.

When he was done, Simon let out a low whistle. "Man, that's rough. What are you going to do?"

"What can I do? She won't take my calls. Blocked my number. She clearly doesn't want to have anything to do with me." Eli took a sip of his scotch and cupped the glass between his hands, staring down into the amber abyss. "I can't believe I'm telling you all this."

"We can't always pick our allies. You know, beggars can't be choosers and all that." Simon tossed back the rest of his drink.

"You have a weird, twisted point." Eli loosened his tie and undid the first button on his shirt. "So how do I win back a woman who won't talk to me? She won't even let me show her the plans for Candy Court."

"What plans?"

Eli set his glass aside and grabbed a cardboard tube from behind his desk. He slid the plans out and spread them flat on the desk. Simon leaned forward to study them for a long minute then sat back, running a finger thoughtfully along his jaw. "Interesting."

"Yep."

"Not our usual M.O."

"Nope."

Simon tapped the plans. "If this doesn't convince her you

love her, nothing will."

"That would be great if there were a snowball's chance in hell I could get her to look at it."

"You need to find out where she's going to be. Somewhere public, where she can't freak out. Then you spring this on her, say those three magic words, and bam. All is forgiven."

"Sounds kind of like stalking."

"Not if it works," Simon shot back, unruffled. "Then it's romantic."

Eli drummed his fingers on the desktop, something he did when he was deep in thought. "She mentioned something about a neighborhood meeting to discuss the sale of the building."

"Perfect." Simon raised his glass, signaling for a refill. "Women love a grand gesture. You can unveil the plans there. Win everyone over with your wit, charm, and brilliant vision."

"It's pretty risky," Eli mused, ignoring his friend's empty glass. "What if she turns me down? I'm not really into public humiliation."

"What's that old saying? Nothing ventured, nothing gained?" Giving up on Eli, Simon went to the credenza and poured his own drink. "You didn't get where you are today by playing it safe."

Eli lifted his glass to his lips and drank, a plan already starting to form. He'd have to move fast. First order of business was to find out when and where the meeting was being held without tipping off Brooke. And he knew just the person to help him.

"Go big or go home." He raised his glass in a mock toast.

Simon clinked his glass with Eli's. "Exactly."

...

Working from home had its advantages. Like not showering

for days on end and subsisting on junk food and Diet Coke. Made wallowing in self-pity so much easier.

It helped that Brooke had a little sister willing to overlook her substandard appearance—and questionable odor—and trek out to Brooklyn to replenish her supply of said junk food and Diet Coke.

"Thanks, Mal." Brooke took one of the grocery bags from her sister, brought it over to the counter, and started to unpack. Powdered donuts. Chex mix. Slim Jims. Twinkies. It looked like Mallory had bought out an entire gas station convenience store.

Their parents were right. She was the nice one.

"I brought some real food, too, so you don't die of malnutrition." Mallory followed Brooke into the apartment and hip-checked the door closed behind her, her arms otherwise occupied with the remaining grocery bag. "And a little something special."

She dangled a smaller plastic bag from her fingers. Brooke took it from her and peered inside.

"Please tell me that's your homemade black satin mousse cake inside that box," she said hopefully.

"If the kitchen at the Worthington counts as home." Mallory put the second grocery bag on the counter along with her purse and leaned against it to scrutinize her sister. "That's an interesting ensemble."

"What, this old thing?" Brooke fingered the hem of her tattered RISD sweatshirt, which she'd paired with Minnie Mouse pajama pants and fluffy unicorn slippers.

"And you smell god-awful." Mallory wrinkled her nose. "How long has it been since you showered?"

So much for overlooking her lack of personal hygiene. "I plead the fifth."

"I get that you're nursing a broken heart." Her sister reached into the second grocery bag and started pulling out what she apparently considered real food. Baby carrots. Hummus. Chicken cutlets. Bananas. "But you're going to have to leave this apartment eventually."

"Eventually can be a long, long time." With the bags unpacked, Brooke got to work putting the perishables in the refrigerator.

"What about the bar? Don't they need you?"

"I've been cutting back on my hours there, working on my book and doing more freelance design stuff."

"That's good, I guess." Mallory picked up a banana, peeled it, and took a bite. "But you're going to have to rejoin the land of the living at some point. You're not the first person to be unlucky in love."

"More than unlucky, Mal." Brooke put the last of the perishables in the refrigerator, closed the door, and slumped against it. "He lied to me. About everything. Our entire relationship was one big, colossal joke to him."

"You don't know that."

"I know the whole time he was screwing me, he was planning on evicting me."

"Do you?" Mallory asked. "He said he was buying the building, but did he tell you what he was going to do with it?"

"Not exactly," Brooke hedged. "But he's a big-time real estate developer. It doesn't take a rocket scientist to figure out that he's going to tear this place to the ground and put up a luxury high-rise. Or convert it into overpriced condos for the nouveau riche."

"I'll admit, it doesn't look good." Mallory polished off the banana and threw the peel in the trash. "But didn't he give you some kind of explanation when you asked him?"

"I didn't ask." Brooke tore open the bag of Chex mix and dug in.

Mallory nodded knowingly. "Now I'm getting the picture. You did your cut-and-run routine."

What was she talking about? Brooke was all fight, not flight. "I do not cut and run."

"You don't think you do, but you do." Mallory pulled a stool out from under the counter and sat. "Why else would you be living way out here?"

Brooke took a seat on the stool across from her, putting the bag of Chex mix between them. "It's Brooklyn, Mal. Not Bosnia."

"Might as well be." Mallory grabbed a handful of Chex mix and popped some into her mouth. "Look, I'm not saying running is always a bad thing. Sometimes a little distance is healthy. Necessary, even. It's something I've been thinking about a lot lately."

A soft, faraway look came into her sister's eyes, and Brooke wondered what she was hinting at. It disappeared as quickly as it came. The moment passed, and Mallory continued. "But before you head for the metaphorical hills, you should at least give Eli a chance to tell his side of the story."

"His side of the story?" Brooke almost choked on her Chex mix. "He lied. What more is there to know?"

"Didn't you lie, too? Or did you tell him you're Brooke Worthington of the hotel Worthingtons?"

Snagged.

"It's not the same." Brooke broke open the box of donuts, took one out and all but inhaled it. Two thumbs up for emotional eating.

"Isn't it? At least a little bit?" Mallory didn't wait for her to answer. "You owe him the chance to explain. You owe it to yourself."

"How can you be so sure?" Brooke licked powdered sugar off her lip. "What do you know that I don't?"

"I watched you two at the wedding. I haven't seen you that happy and relaxed with a member of the opposite sex in, like, ever. And that guy is totally in love with you. He couldn't take his eyes off you all night."

Something stirred inside her. Something she didn't want to acknowledge, much less name. She pushed it way down deep and reached for another donut. "You got all that from a few hours on a rooftop in questionable lighting?"

Mallory hopped off her stool and grabbed two Diet Cokes out of the refrigerator. "Sometimes you've just got to trust your instincts."

She kept one of the sodas for herself and slid the other across the counter to Brooke. Then she sat back down, popped the tab, and drank.

Brooke followed suit, wiping her mouth on the sleeve of her sweatshirt when she was done. "Yeah, well, my instincts suck. They let me fall in love with someone who's a carbon copy of Dad."

"Really? Aside from the fact that he's one of the richest men in Manhattan, how is Eli remotely like Dad?"

"He's..." Brooke stalled. How was Eli like her father? He was supportive, not selfish. Took an interest in her career, her friends. Fixed sinks and planned weddings without asking for or expecting anything in return. And although he was rich, he didn't let his money define him.

Qualities as foreign to her father as making minimum wage.

Mallory cleared her throat. "I'm waiting."

Since Brooke had no answer to her sister's question, she asked one of her own. "How do I know it wasn't all an act?"

"You don't." Mallory gave a rueful little lift of her shoulder. "Not for certain. That's where those instincts come in. And yours aren't anywhere near as bad as you think. You had Hunter pegged as a pretentious prick the minute you met him."

Brooke's jaw dropped, and a little piece of donut plopped

onto her sweatshirt just above her left breast. "I never said..."

"You didn't have to," Mallory interrupted. "It was written all over your face. And you were right. We broke up."

"Oh, Mal." Brooke reached across the counter and covered Mallory's hand with hers. "I'm sorry. I've been so preoccupied with my own drama, I didn't realize you were hurting, too."

"Probably because I'm not." Mallory gave her sister's hand a reassuring squeeze. "Which should tell you something."

"What?"

"The man I lost wasn't worth keeping. But maybe—just maybe—yours is."

Mallory's cell phone chimed. She pulled it out of her purse, swiped the screen and scowled.

"What's wrong?" Brooke asked.

Mallory tossed her phone back into her purse and stood. "The idiots at the fish market messed up our delivery again. I've got to go take care of this, or we'll have to take the scallop special off the menu tonight."

"Go. Don't worry about me. I'll be fine here with my processed food and carbonated syrup." Brooke held up her soda can in mock toast.

"Okay. But promise me you'll think about what we discussed."

"I promise." Not a hard one to make. Or to keep. Brooke couldn't imagine she'd have space in her brain for much else.

Mallory came around the counter to give her sister a hug. "And one more thing."

"Name it."

Mallory scrunched up her nose and pulled away. "Take a shower."

Chapter Fifteen

"Not bad for our first meeting." Brooke stood in the back of the gym at the neighborhood elementary school and surveyed the crowd filing in and taking their seats in the folding chairs she, Charise, and David had spent the last hour setting up. They were lucky the school board had agreed to let them use the space. They would have been spilling out the door of Brooke's studio. "I'd say we've got at least a hundred people out there."

"Just wait." Charise rubbed her hands together. "We'll have a bigger crowd next meeting when we've got more time to get the word out. We're not going down without a fight."

"The natives are getting restless." Brooke shuffled the papers in her folder. "We should get things rolling."

"No," David squeaked, bouncing on the balls of his feet. "Not yet. It's still a few minutes before seven."

Brooke eyed him suspiciously. "What is with you?"

"Nothing." He stopped bouncing and stuffed his hands into the pockets of his perfectly pressed khakis. "I just think we should give everyone a chance to get here. We need all the help we can get."

"Okay, you win. I'm going to find a quiet corner to go over my notes." A little extra prep time couldn't hurt. Just as she'd predicted, she'd been distracted since her sister's visit, Mallory's words continuously bumping around her brain.

That guy is totally in love with you.

You owe him the chance to explain. You owe it to yourself.

Sometimes you've just got to trust your instincts.

Like that was so easy. Her instincts were what had gotten her into this mess in the first place. Out of all the guys in the five boroughs, leave it to her to pick the one buying her building to be her one-night stand. A one-night stand that had morphed into something much, much more.

She'd thought about calling Eli a hundred million trillion times. But each time she picked up the phone, she put it back down again. He'd tried to reach out to her in the days following the auction, and she'd shot him down at every turn. What if it was too late now? What if she put her heart on the line only to find out he'd moved on? That he no longer cared about her or Candy Court?

Brooke shook her head to clear it. She didn't have time for this now. She needed to bring her A game tonight. The rest of Candy Court—the rest of the neighborhood—was counting on her. At least she'd showered and put on pants without an elastic waistband and a shirt that didn't advertise what she'd eaten for dinner last night. That was a step in the right direction.

She clutched her folder to her chest and headed for the hallway. She needed out of the gym, with its noisy buzz of chatter and the heat building up as the crowd grew. "Come get me when you're ready to start."

David found her ten minutes later in a classroom across the hall, still reviewing her notes. Zoning laws. Variances. Historical landmarks. There was a lot to remember, every bit of it important if they were going to save their homes and the area around them.

"You're on." He gave her a thumbs-up then let his cheerful guard down, his eyes filling with concern. "Are you sure you're up for this?"

"I'm sure." With shaky hands, she put her papers back in the folder, checking and double-checking that they were in the right order. "I know I'll have to face him sooner or later, but it's not like he's going to be here tonight."

David was the only one at Candy Court who she'd told about Eli buying the building. Probably because, other than her sister, he was the only one brave enough to get close to her when she looked and smelled like yesterday's garbage. The others just thought Eli had gone as quickly and mysteriously as he'd come.

They'd find out the truth soon enough. She didn't want to be the one to disillusion them.

"Right." David pulled on his collar. "Let's go."

The gym was more crowded now. Brooke recognized a few familiar faces in addition to the Candy Court crew. Her boss and some of the other staff at Flotsam and Jetsam. The two guys who owned the brewpub. Wayne, looking clean and sober with a middle-aged woman she assumed was his wife.

"Good turnout," David observed as they climbed the stairs to the stage at the far end of the gym, where Charise and the Feingolds were seated.

"What's the holdup?" Mr. Feingold grumbled. "I want to get to the cookies and coffee."

"Like you need cookies," his wife shot back. "And you know you're not supposed to have caffeine after eight o'clock, or you'll never get to sleep."

Brooke stepped up to the microphone front and center. "If you'll take your seats, we'll get started."

She waited a minute for everyone to get settled before

she began. "As you know, we're here to discuss the sale of Candy Court and what it means for our community."

"It means we're going to be the next Park Slope," someone shouted out.

"And pretty soon none of us will be able to afford to live in our own neighborhood," someone else added.

"That's what we're here to prevent," Brooke said. "I have a few ideas…"

"If we let them take Candy Court, who's going to come in next?"

"Our small businesses can't compete against the big chains."

Brooke tightened her grip on the microphone stand. "If we could all raise our hands…"

"What do we know about this development group?"

"Do we have any idea what they have planned for the building?"

Okay, so hand-raising was out. "No. Not yet. But…"

"Actually, yes, we do."

For a second, Brooke thought she was hallucinating. It wasn't out of the realm of possibility. She'd been hearing Eli's voice in her head for weeks. His sexy growl. The way he cried out her name as he climaxed. But it usually started up when her head hit the pillow and she tried in vain to sleep, not in moments of full, waking consciousness. She hadn't gone that far off the deep end. Yet.

Then she saw him, striding down the center aisle with a cardboard tube tucked under his arm, moving like he owned the goddamn world.

Why did he always have to look so good? If there were any justice in the world, he'd look as bad as she felt. Bloodshot eyes. Scraggly hair. At least some three-day-old scruff on his jaw.

But no. Eli was bright-eyed, neatly coiffed, and clean

shaven, looking like he stepped out of the pages of *Esquire* or *GQ* in what must be business casual for him—a crisp, white button-down shirt, lightweight gray cardigan, and dark jeans.

He climbed up onto the stage, exchanging hugs with a squealing Charise and an equally excited Mrs. Feingold and a fist bump with her more reserved husband. Then he motioned to David, who scrambled to set up an easel he'd procured from who knew where.

"You were in on this, weren't you?" Brooke glared at David, who merely shrugged as he struggled with the easel. "Traitor."

She wheeled on Eli, who was so close she felt like she was drowning in the scent of him, fresh soap mixed with spicy cologne. She tried to ignore the tingling sensation in her nether regions. "And you. You're just as bad, showing up here without any warning."

"You didn't leave me much choice. Wouldn't take my calls. Didn't answer my texts. It was the only way I could think of to get you to listen to me."

Okay. She'd give him that one. "And you had to do it in front of half the neighborhood?"

There was that drop-your-panties smile that made her stupid. "Less chance you'd run."

Again with the running? Did everyone think she was afraid of confrontation?

"Besides," he continued, waving an arm at the crowd below, who watched the proceedings with interest. "This concerns them, too."

He pulled a sheet of paper from the tube and taped it up to the easel. She studied it over his shoulder, not quite believing what she was seeing. Where was the glossy high-rise? Where were the three-thousand-square-foot luxury condos?

"What's this?"

"My plans for the Sunset Park Chocolate Works."

"What's the Chocolate Works?" someone asked.

"Good question," Eli said, taking over the microphone. "First, let me introduce myself. I'm Eli Ward from Hearthstone Development, the new owner of the Sunset Park Chocolate Works, formerly Candy Court."

"Great, he's changing the name," someone grumbled from below.

"What else are you going to change?" someone else asked, louder. Other voices joined in, and the hum of the crowd rose to a dull roar.

Eli seemed unfazed. "I suggest we adjourn for a few minutes. Give everyone a chance to come up and have a look at the plans. Then I'll be happy to answer any questions you might have."

He put his hand over the mic and turned to Brooke. "And you and I can discuss this in private."

She stared at him for a long, awkward moment, weighing her options. It was decision time. Open up to hurt or walk away. Finally, she pushed his hand away from the microphone and leaned in.

"Meeting adjourned."

• • •

Meeting adjourned.

Funny how two little words could make his heart soar.

Eli grabbed Brooke by the hand and dragged her off the stage before she had time to change her mind. Once in the hall, he pushed open the first door he found, which of course, turned out to be a supply closet, this time stocked with glue sticks and markers and pencils as round as his thumb.

"What is it with you and closets?" Brooke rested her perfect ass on a shelf of spiral notebooks. "Do you have a fetish or something?"

Eli willed himself to focus on the speech he'd rehearsed a thousand times on the way to Brooklyn. He had one shot to get this right, and he wasn't going to waste it. Even if it meant having one of the most important conversations of his life in a closet.

Again.

She gave him a don't-bullshit-me glare and crossed her arms. "You've got five minutes."

Okay. She wasn't going to make it easy on him. He couldn't say that he blamed her.

He braced a hand against the door. "I'm sorry. I was wrong to keep you in the dark about Candy Court."

She smirked. "Tell me something I don't know."

"I thought I could wait until the sale was a lock. I didn't want to leave anything up to chance. I've lost a few deals recently at the eleventh hour, and I didn't want that to happen again."

"So you could make a small fortune turning our building into a haven for yuppies and elitists?"

"At first, yes, that was the plan." She bristled, and his heart started to pound. He couldn't afford to lose her now, not when he was just getting to the good part. "But that changed once I moved in and got to know you. All of you."

"So those drawings out there..."

"They're the real deal," he insisted. "The only thing that's going to change at Candy Court is the name. Well, that and some upgrades. All in keeping with the history and character of the building, of course."

"No luxury condos?"

"Studio apartments, one bedrooms, maybe a handful of two bedrooms for families. Quality, affordable housing for hard-working, middle-class people. That's what Hearthstone is going to be all about."

"What about Momentum?"

"Simon will make sure Momentum keeps doing what it does best. High-end commercial development. Hearthstone's my baby."

"You've really put a lot of thought into this."

He took a step toward her, and his spirits lifted when she didn't flinch. "Did you seriously think I could throw the Feingolds out on the street? Or Charise and her baby? And I'm not about to destroy the rooftop garden we worked so hard on. Chris and David would never speak to me again."

She lifted one eyebrow, a gesture that was incongruously both imperious and endearing. "Aren't you leaving someone out?"

"Not just someone." He reached up to touch her face. "*The* one."

"Not so fast." She caught his hand and brought it down. "I haven't forgiven you."

His heart stuttered. "What do you think it'll take?"

"Well, let's see." She kept hold of his hand, twining her fingers with his, and his heart kick-started into high gear. "You've admitted you were wrong."

"Check."

"Said you were sorry."

"Check."

"Hmm." She titled her head thoughtfully. "What else could there be?"

Shit. The three little words.

"I'm an idiot." Not exactly the three words he was going for, but they were the ones that spilled out.

"You're not an idiot." She let out a strangled laugh. "I take that back. You are kind of an idiot for thinking your money would color my perception of you. But it's not like I can throw stones."

"Ah, yes. Brooke Worthington, heiress."

She winced and relaxed her hand, letting his fingers slide

through hers. "You know."

He nodded. "I didn't expect to see you at the auction that night. Of course, maybe if I had realized it was at your family's hotel…"

"I never meant to mislead you. It just never seemed important. And it's not something I like to discuss." She blushed and ducked her head, her dark tresses shadowing her face. "I guess we both made mistakes."

"Me more than you," he admitted. "Is it too late to fix them?"

She raised her chin and faced him head on, her green eyes clear and honest, hiding nothing. Now he understood that whole windows-to-the-soul thing. "We'll never know until we try."

He took a deep breath and stuck out his hand. "Hi. I'm Eli Ward. I'm filthy rich, and I'm buying the building you live in, but I promise not to tear it down, kick you out, or raise your rent. Oh, and I'm truly, madly, deeply, irrevocably in love with you."

Slowly, carefully, like she was about to touch a live wire, she took his hand, her fingers curling into the warmth of his. "Hi. I'm Brooke Worthington. My family owns a bunch of hotels, and I was raised in the lap of luxury, but that's not really my scene. And I'm truly, deeply, madly, irrevocably in love with you, too."

"Thank God." He pulled her in and crushed her to him, relief swelling his chest. "I was hoping you meant it when you said you loved me in that closet at the Worthington. Hoping I hadn't fucked it all up beyond repair."

"You came close." She smiled against his throat. "But lucky for you, I'm a forgiving kind of gal."

"I can't promise not to fuck up again." He slid a finger under her chin and lifted her head. "But I can promise not to keep anything from you. No more secrets."

"No more secrets," she repeated on a shaky breath.

His hand went around to the back of her neck, and his lips brushed hers in a soft, tender kiss that, laced with two weeks of unrequited longing, almost immediately turned passionate. Their mouths clashed as he moved against her, backing her up against the wall of shelves. No shrinking violet, Brooke demanded equal participation, her hands moving up to her shoulders, digging into his shirt and tugging him closer.

He kissed her long and hard and deep, their breath coming hot and fast, until he heard a high-pitched, girlish giggle. When they pulled apart, Mrs. Feingold and Charise stood in the doorway, beaming at them.

"Don't mind us," the older woman said, already closing the door. "You just keep doing what you're doing."

"Although, you might want to wrap it up and save it for later," Charise suggested. "There's a gym full of people waiting to hear about your plans for the Chocolate Works."

"You know," Brooke said when the door had swung shut, her breath still coming in staccato pants, "this could be a thing for us."

"A thing?" He nuzzled her neck.

"Yeah." She reached up to stroke his hair. "All our declarations of love take place in a closet."

"No way." He raised his head, needing her to see the sincerity in his eyes when he spoke. "I fully intend to tell you I love you wherever and whenever I damn well please."

She wrapped her arms around his waist and smiled up at him. "I can live with that."

"Good." His lips returned to her neck. "Now, where were we?"

She laughed and pushed him away. "Hold it right there, Mr. One Track Mind. You heard Charise. You've got a room full of people waiting on you."

"Waiting on us," he corrected. "None of this would

possible be if it wasn't for you."

"Then let's not keep them waiting." She held out a hand to him. "The sooner we show them your brilliant ideas and convince them you're not going to run them out of their neighborhood, the sooner we can go home and pick up where we left off."

Home. He had plans for that, too. Ones he'd share with Brooke when the time was right. For now, it was enough that she was his and he was hers.

And if that wasn't a damn good reason for him to feel like the luckiest man in the word, he didn't know what was.

Epilogue

"Hey, Brooke." David poked his head in the door of the fifth-floor apartment she shared with Eli. Without knocking, of course. "Chris needs you on the roof."

She finished shading a panel of her newest graphic novel, the sequel to the one her agent had finally sold, and set her pencil down against the lip of her drawing table. "It's like thirty degrees out. What's he doing up there?"

"He said something about checking on the cold frames." David held his hands palms-up in a how-the-heck-should-I-know gesture. "I think he's worried the clematis won't make it through another frost."

"He can handle that by himself. What does he need me for? Is there some sort of problem?"

"I'm not sure, Miss Twenty Questions. All I know is if I don't get you up there ASAP, I'm going to have one pissed-off husband on my hands. And a pissed-off husband means little Davey doesn't get any action tonight."

Brooke rolled her neck and stretched her arms above her head. Maybe a little break was just what she needed. She'd been hunched over her drawing table for hours, trying to finish the chapter she was working on before Eli came home from his business trip. He'd been gone four days, and the three-bedroom, two-and-a-half bath apartment he'd specially designed for them when he finished off the top floors of the Chocolate Works seemed like a tomb without him.

She stood and stretched again, releasing her hair from the ponytail she always wore when she was drawing and shaking it out. "Far be it from me to stand in the way of little Davey's sexual gratification. Let me grab my coat, and I'll meet Chris up there."

"Fine. But don't take too long. Little Davey…"

"I know, I know. Little Davey needs to get some."

David gave her a thumbs-up and disappeared. Brooke wandered down the hall to the master bedroom to dig up a jacket, dodging unpacked bags and boxes as she went. They'd only been in the apartment a few weeks. Eli had busted his ass to get the renovations done in record time. Probably because he'd sold his penthouse and was tired of sharing a tiny bathroom with Brooke and all her bottles and tubes and jars.

She'd told him he was nuts, but he insisted he was sick of living downtown and didn't want to wait until the renovations were complete to start their life together. He said he'd miss waking up with her, but Brooke had a sneaking suspicion there were other things he'd miss, too. Like Mrs. Feingold's rugelach, sampling local craft beers with David and Chris after the latter returned from his tour, and roughhousing with little Jaden, who was just starting to walk. He might not want to admit it out loud, but Eli was as much a part of the Candy Court crew as her.

Brooke grabbed the first outer garment she could find—Eli's leather bomber jacket—and slipped it on, pausing to bury her face in the collar and inhale the smell of the well-worn leather mixed with his cologne. Four days. That was all he'd been gone. So why did it seem like four freaking years?

Because she'd turned into a certified, card-carrying, make-you-wanna-puke, hopeless romantic, that was why. The kind of girl who smelled her boyfriend's jacket. Wore his shirts. Slept clutching his pillow when he out of town.

And she'd never been happier.

She shoved her keys in her pocket and closed the door behind her, testing the handle to make sure it was locked. She still wasn't the greatest at the whole door-locking thing, but Eli made her promise she'd be more careful now that new tenants were starting to move into the building. The least she could do was secure the place when she left.

"All right, Chris," she called to her friend as she pushed her way through the door to the roof. "You got me up here. Now, what was so important that..."

Her voice trailed off as she absorbed the scene in front of her. Eli stood under a tent like the one he'd set up for Chris and David's wedding, complete with twinkling LEDs and two portable space heaters chugging away to ward off the winter chill. A round table just the right size for an intimate meal sat dead center, flanked by two comfortable looking wicker chairs with puffy, off-white cushions. The table was draped with a matching gauzy, off-white cloth, on top of which sat two elegant place settings and a bottle of wine chilling in a shining silver ice bucket.

"I thought you weren't due back until tomorrow." Hello, mouth, meet foot. When your boyfriend surprised you with a romantic rooftop dinner date, you were supposed to leap into his arms and kiss him stupid, not ask him what the hell he was doing there. She still had a lot to learn about this relationship stuff. Fortunately, Eli was a patient teacher.

"Nice to see you, too." His broad smile took any sting out of his words. He gestured to the chair opposite him. "Join me?"

Brooke arched a brow. "What would you do if I said no?"

"Rumor has it Mrs. Feingold is available. It's her husband's bowling night."

"Yeah, but can Mrs. Feingold do this?" She crossed to him, took his head in her hands, and pulled it to her waiting lips. After a stunned second, he reciprocated, snaking an arm around her waist to tug her body tight to his. She sighed and relaxed into him, loving the way they fit together, her soft curves yielding to his rigid angles. That was something she didn't think she'd ever get tired of.

When they'd finished making up for four whole days spent with half a continent between them, they drew apart. Eli gave her that lopsided, impish grin of his that even after almost a year together never failed to turn her insides to mush. "If Mrs. Feingold can do that, I sure as hell don't want to find out."

Brooke returned his smile with a playful one of her own. "What's wrong? Little old ladies not your type?"

"You're my type." He gave her a swift, sizzling kiss, turned her around, and with a pat on her bottom nudged her toward the nearest chair, which he pulled out for her. "Sit."

She studied the picture-perfect setting Eli had clearly worked hard to create then glanced back at the man responsible, noticing for the first time his neatly pressed dress pants and cranberry V-neck cashmere sweater rolled at the sleeves, the starched, white collar and cuffs of his dress shirt peeking out from underneath. She frowned down at her frayed yoga pants and well-worn, much loved Cowboy Bebop T-shirt, partially covered by Eli's half-zipped bomber jacket, which swallowed up her shoulders and hung past her hips. If she'd known what was in store for her, she would have taken a couple of minutes to throw on something decent and freshen up. "I feel underdressed."

"You look beautiful. Stop stalling and sit down."

She obeyed, and he poured them each a glass of chardonnay before taking his seat across from her. Seemingly out of nowhere, David appeared at his side dressed entirely in black, the only splash of color a bright red napkin draped over one arm. "Are you ready for the first course?"

"First course?" She blinked. "How many are there?"

"Yes," Eli said, directing his answer at David and ignoring Brooke. "Thank you."

With an exaggerated bow, David disappeared as silently as he'd come. Brooke shook her head. "Who else did you rope into this? Please tell me Mr. Feingold's not going to show up when he's done bowling and serenade us with his accordion."

"Nope. Just you, me, and our hopefully unobtrusive waiter from here on in."

Eli raised his glass in a toast. She lifted hers in response, and they clinked them together then sipped.

She tilted her head and gazed at him over the rim of her glass. "What's the special occasion?"

He shrugged and took another sip of his chardonnay. "Who says we need one?

"We don't. But knowing you, there's something I'm forgetting."

"All right, if you must know." He traced the rim of his glass with his index finger. "It's our one-year anniversary."

She pursed her lips. "I may not be the world's best girlfriend, but I know we didn't start officially dating until after the Geek Girls benefit. And that was in April, not January."

"Not that anniversary." He set his glass down and reached across the table to take her hand. "The anniversary of the night we met. In the back room at Flotsam and Jetsam."

"We didn't exactly meet in the back room." She shivered as he drew slow circles with his thumb on her palm. Leave it to Eli to memorialize their one-night stand that wasn't. The guy had a seriously secret sentimental side and a dirty mind he kept equally under wraps with everyone but her.

"Maybe not." One corner of his mouth curled into a naughty grin. "But it was certainly the most memorable part of the evening."

David reappeared, humming Beethoven's Moonlight Sonata and bearing two steaming soup bowls, about as unobtrusive as an elephant in a tutu.

"Roast carrot and fennel soup with parsley walnut pesto," he announced as he set the bowls down in front of them.

"Looks delish," Brooke said, digging in.

Eli chuckled, and she paused with her spoon halfway to her mouth. "What's so funny?"

"You. It's refreshing to see a woman who's not afraid to enjoy her food." He laid his spoon aside and cleared his throat. "I was going to wait until dessert, but…"

He pushed his chair back and fumbled in his pants pocket. "Dammit. Things went a lot smoother when I imagined this moment. But I was afraid to lose it, so I pinned it to the lining."

"Afraid to lose what?"

"This."

Brooke's heart stuttered to a stop. Between the thumb and index finger of his outstretched hand, Eli held the most exquisite diamond ring she'd ever seen. The shimmering, old European cut diamond was set in platinum and accented on either side by a trio of smaller, single-cut stones, giving the ring a vintage, art deco feel.

She sat transfixed, unable to move but eventually, thankfully, able to speak. "Does that mean what I think?"

"If you think it means I'm asking you to spend the rest of your life with me, 'til death do us part, then yes." The silence stretched between them as he twirled the ring in his fingers, the light from the LEDs catching the facets of the stones in brilliant, golden flashes. "I believe it's customary for the lady to give some sort of an answer."

"Well, duh." She plucked the ring from his fingers and slipped it over her knuckle, resisting the urge to go all girly and stretch out her hand to admire it. There was time enough for that later, in private. "Of course I'll marry you. Who else would put up with my mood swings, off-key singing, and Diet Coke addiction?"

"A small price to pay for my snoring, leaving the cap off the toothpaste, and neglecting to change the toilet paper roll."

He leaned in to kiss her. She met him halfway, but their lips had barely made contact when a piercing shriek cut through the air, making them jump apart.

"Oh. My. God." David whipped his cell phone out of his pocket and stabbed at the screen. "Houston, we have a problem. Lover boy jumped the gun. She's got the ring on her finger. Get up here with the good stuff, stat."

He ended the call, shoved the phone back in his pocket and glared at Eli. "What happened to waiting for dessert?"

"Sorry." Eli gave one shoulder a half-hearted shrug that said he wasn't the least bit sorry. "Patience isn't my strong suit."

"What does he mean, the good stuff?" Brooke smiled across the table at her fiancé. *Fiancé*. The word sent ripples of excitement and anticipation through her. Eli was her fiancé. She was going to be his wife. A year ago—hell, eight months ago—it would have seemed impossible. But now the impossible had become reality. "I thought this night was pretty darned good already."

"He means this." Chris stepped out onto the roof, brandishing a bottle of what looked like champagne and followed by Charise and the Feingolds. "It was supposed to be for when he popped the question."

"What happened?" Mr. Feingold fiddled with his hearing aid. "Did she say yes?"

"Of course she did," his wife scolded him. "Can't you see

the rock on her finger?"

"This calls for champagne." Chris popped the cork.

"Thanks." Eli took the bottle from him. "I think I can take it from here."

"What about dinner?" David protested. "There's four more courses to go."

Chris nodded in agreement. "You haven't lived until you've tasted my salt encrusted beef tenderloin."

"I'll text you when we're ready for the next course," Eli promised.

"If you want some mood music, I could get my accordion," offered Mr. Feingold.

"Come on, old man." His wife tugged at the sleeve of his cardigan. "The lovebirds want some privacy."

"Mrs. Feingold is right." Charise started for the door. "Let's leave the happy couple alone."

After a bit of grumbling, mostly from Mr. Feingold, the group said their congratulations and left.

Eli pushed back his chair and stood. "Dance with me."

"There's no music."

"Do we need any?" He extended his hand to her. "I want to hold you."

How could a girl resist an invitation like that? Brooke took his hand and let him pull her out of her seat and into his arms.

"You realize my mother's going to be beside herself." She rested her cheek on his shoulder as they moved to the music in their minds. "Her eldest daughter marrying Manhattan's most eligible bachelor? She's going to want a big society wedding, with all the trimmings."

"Is that what you want?" Eli asked.

"Hell, no." She shuddered at the thought. "I just want you."

"That's what I was hoping you'd say." He stopped swaying

to pull an envelope from his back pocket.

"What's this?" she asked, taking it.

"Why don't you open it and find out?"

She broke the seal and slid out two airline tickets. "Costa Rica?"

"I did a little leg work. All you need to get a marriage license is a passport and two witnesses."

"A marriage license?" She gazed up at him, open mouthed. "You mean elope?"

"That's the plan, if you're on board."

She studied the tickets, her lower lip trembling. "This flight leaves in less than twelve hours. I'll never be ready in time."

"Charise is packing your bag as we speak."

Brooke slipped the tickets back into the envelope. "You really did think of everything, didn't you?"

"Yep. All I need now is the girl." He took the envelope from her fingertips, returned it to his pocket and cupped her face in his hands. "What do you say, sweetheart?"

"What do I say?" She laughed, raised herself up on her toes, and kissed him—a long, lingering kiss that communicated her answer in a way words never could. But to be sure, when she was done she gave him the words, too.

"I say you've got her. And we have a plane to catch."

Acknowledgments

No writer is an island, and I couldn't have written this book without a huge support system behind me. There's my plot group, the MTBs, who always have wine, chocolate, and words of condolence or congratulations at the ready, depending on my mood: Jamie Beck, Jamie Schmidt, Megan Ryder, Gail Chianese, Jane Haertel, Jen Moncuse, Stefanie London, Katy Lee, and Tracy Costa. There's my agent, Jill Marsal, who started me on this part of my writing journey when she said, "I think you should submit something to Entangled." There's my editor, Candace Havens, editorial director, Heidi Shoham, and the rest of the staff at Entangled, who've been a delight to work with and who've helped this book get stronger every step of the way. There's my usually understanding husband and daughter, who tolerate way more than their fair share of take-out dinners, dirty dishes, and half-done laundry, not to mention deadline-induced panic.

And last, but by no means least, there's you, the readers. I've had the pleasure of meeting many of you at conferences, signings, and author/reader weekends. Trust me, it never gets old. You're the reason authors write, and without you we're just shouting into the wind. Thanks for letting me share Brooke and Eli's story with you.

About the Author

Regina Kyle also writes for Harlequin Blaze. She is a 2016 Booksellers' Best Winner (*Triple Dare*—Erotic Romance) and a 2015 NJRW Golden Leaf Finalist (*Triple Threat*—Best First Book). Regina knew she was destined to be an author when she won a writing contest at age ten with a touching tale about a squirrel and a nut pie. By day, she writes dry legal briefs, representing the state in criminal appeals. At night, she writes steamy romance with heart and humor. A lover of all things theatrical, Regina lives on the Connecticut coast with her husband, teenage daughter, and two melodramatic cats. When she's not writing, she's most likely singing, reading, cooking, or watching bad reality television. She's a member of Romance Writers of America and of her local RWA chapter.

Discover more category romance titles from Entangled Indulgence...

The Baby Project

a *Kingston Family* novel by Miranda Liasson

Liz Kingston spends her life delivering babies and longs for one of her own. Who better to ask than her sexy ex-fling, who has no interest in ever settling down or being a father. Nothing in all of international correspondent Grant Wilbanks's experience could have prepared him for the way a torrid affair with Liz makes him feel. When she asks for his assistance, he figures he can help her out with a simple donation. No strings, no emotions, just...test-tube science. But this simple favor gives them both more than they ever bargained for.

The Billionaire's Paradise

a *Sexy Billionaires* novel by Victoria Davies

Billionaire Hayden Wexton wants one more night with consultant Avery Clarke while she uses her expertise to saves his resort. He doesn't understand why they can't mix a little business with pleasure. One more night, and maybe he can finally get her out of his head. Avery wanted to enjoy her working vacation. But Hayden seriously interrupts that bliss. Unfortunately, Hayden isn't a man to offer anything more than a vacation fling, and Avery has no intention of becoming another name on his list of broken hearts. Even if the man might just be the best mistake she's ever made.

The Billionaire's Private Scandal

an *Invested in Love* novel by Jenna Bayley-Burke

When Megan's secret lover betrays her and steals her family's hotel business, she's grateful no one knew they were involved. It's almost like the relationship and breakup never happened... except for her broken heart. Brandon Knight can't understand why the woman of his dreams disappeared without any explanation. When he finds her working in a coffee shop, he realizes she's got the situation—and him—all wrong. Now all he has to do is prove it.

The Mistaken Billionaire

a *Muse* novel by Lexxie Couper

When a mysterious woman shows up at Thomas St Clair's door and her presence drives away his writer's block, he's willing to put up with her secrets if it means she'll stay around. Mila Elderkin once had a promising career in journalism, until her dreams were shattered by a rising star in the literary world. When fate lands her at that same man's door years later, and he doesn't recognize her, it seems she's been offered a chance for a little fun. But the past has funny way of creeping into the present, and secrets don't lie quiet forever.

Made in the USA
Middletown, DE
23 September 2021